Scattered Green Galaxies Publishing

Falls Church, Va 22042

Copyright 2016

Publication Data

2nd Edition

Barr, Rachel

Spine/ Rachel Barr

----Science Fiction----Dystopian Fiction

ISBN-13:9780991199204

ISBN-10:0991199200

BISAC: Fiction/Dystopian/ Post-Apocalyptic

SPINE

Rachel Barr

Dedicated to Toye,
Max & Jake
& Hanna D.

❧ Prologue

In the dream, she was drowning on dry land.
In the desert of her mind, she was suffocating.
Wordless whispers blew tumbleweed thoughts.
Brush branches skidded across cracked dirt,
Scratching schizoid symbols, signifying nothing.

She stumbled and grazed her knuckles.
Sand sheared her face.
Her last words choked through the endless deadscape,
"I have no one to give my story to."

Just before she woke up, she heard a voice whisper,
"Slip inside the mouth of time and speak to other ages."

❧The Museum, Ages Ago

The museum stood gleaming, obsidian black against a cloudless sky. As all museums do, it housed the past. It housed the things humans did not use anymore, but loved enough to keep around in the attic of time. It towered over the landscape and sprawled across acres, in a remote area cleared for this commissioned purpose.

The museum was a monstrosity; it was supposed to be a beacon of the past and a celebration of the future. It contained an original paper edition of every great printed work. Each of these works had been carefully archived in a massive set of digital files at the behest of a government-bid contract. Predictably, the corporation selected to build this museum had been the lowest bidder.

They had saved money by using Heliod resin glue throughout the structure. Heliod Resin Glue is a wonderful adhesive, however, it is also highly flammable, and not to mention, an extremely volatile substance in its gaseous state, but it is astonishingly cheap. To meet the deadline, and also coincidentally to take advantage of the limited-time sales offer, people rushed to turn in their paper books and set up their electronic file book accounts, which were free at paper book recycling centers. In exchange, they got access to the sky-files, enormous databases that claimed to have almost every book ever made.

In the time it took to build this museum, every book deemed non-essential was recycled as pulp layers for this structure, held in place by the Heliod Resin Glue.

The dedication ceremony for the Paper Book Museum was a week away. That ceremony would never happen.

At this very moment, the museum was, in fact, seconds away from being blown off the face of the planet. Two women with short, brown hair took a last look at the structure through binoculars. They were wearing blast suits and standing on a platform miles away from the future hole in the ground. One of the women jotted notes on a digital paper that she was forced to use due to the lack of paper products available. She nodded to the woman next to her, and they both donned blast hoods.

Both of these women had brown hair. They both had numbers tattooed on their right ankles. Neither their current fame nor their future infamy concerned them. They stood resolute in the stiff wind that cuffed and pushed at their protective suits. In their hands, they each held a detonator-which they pressed.

The explosion broke the calm of the early dawn, blasting dust a mile high into the air. The flash tore through the miles of building and rendered it to powder. Smoke mushroomed up, forming a gleaming cloud of cinders.

Two curious things shot forth in the chaos. The first was a small chunk of porcelain inlaid with gold. It was probably part of the museum's digital toilets. It heaved up and slammed into the earth, at the outer edge of the toxic blast radius; it would serve as the only other testament that a building ever existed. The open, jaw-like wound torn in the earth, patiently waited to swallow the ashes that would gather and settle for decades.

The second thing that spewed forth, from deep underground in the permafrost, was an arboreal spore. It rose up and lofted across the planet, and within a year, this rogue fungus decimated every tree on the planet. It not only killed trees, but every leaf, seed, and even dead paper was not free from this contaminant-they were all subject to what was dubbed the Dry Death, crumbling even the hardiest of cardstock to a harsh yellow dust. Trees and paper were no more. An unintended consequence of the blast. An unintended consequence of the women who saw the need to cause the explosion.

But for now, on the very moment it all began, as the greyblack cloud rolled out in waves from the explosion point, one of the brown-haired women, members of clandestine lobbying and activist group called Consourcium, whispered to the other, "All things flow from Source."

Decades later, one of the bombers, dying of late-stage cancer, gave her final words on the subject, *"We sinned. Rather, I have done so in our name. In the beginning, they reviled us, but now we are known only as our enemies have portrayed us, this fear of our kind holds the public with such mythic force-that we have now become myths ourselves. We sought to protect. Only to save what was taken."*

There is another entry in this data file. It was updated centuries later by an unknown Spine acolyte in the Year of the Thinbanana, date unknown. *"The Spine, were the descendants of the original Consourcium Group. They were right to fear, a* little *knowledge. All things flow from Source."*

🌶 Precisely Present Day, Year of the Thinbanana

Kenda was tall. Just another whip-thin girl flitting around Coffee!!Houses and MeetingPlaces blending in, with her taut red cut of a mouth. She had chopped light green and black nanophoton hair with a reptilian-overlay. She was constantly tugging at her dark green shawl, as it kept slipping off her shoulders. Most of her seemed to shrug off the world entire, paper-thin, yet she persisted to exist though the world barely skipped a breath.

This day , the same as any other, was primarily spent sipping Drink*Coffee!* and sending out messages and pairing the formulaic combinations of silky and smooth and skin and shine, Funlight and friends and fun, Thinbanana and thin, happy people to earn her keep.

As an Information Pairing student at Banburn University, she had the same goal as all of the other Info-Pairing interns-to become a Newsporter. As a Newsporter, her housing, foodstuffs, hair and self-tucking overlay maintenance would be permanently paid for, as long as she kept up her quota of sends, pairing product and emotions and resending them to others.

Kenda was an excellent pairer; she paired with ease, taglines of products and their intersecting emotions. It was partly due to her pairing studies, but with her speed, she was easily one of the most promising students since Kitty Reed went through Banburn U. She had learned early on that the trick of pairing was to pair correctly, pair quickly and tagline each send to earn more Brandsponsors. She already had twelve, including Skinshine and Thinbanana. Only Kitty Reed had ever surpassed that number at her age. Most people were merely Receivers, or non-pairers, and they earned credits on a much smaller scale from special allowances from Brandsponsors. They had to pay for their own hair coloring, food and housing, and Personal Electronic Autonomous Relays, called P_ear consoles. P_ears came either as wrist units or embedded skull units.

Kenda was one of the chosen-an elite core of young people capable of easily connecting pre-made phrases to things and emotion and people- an invaluable skill to possess in the economy of advertisers. For just a few hundred sends a day, she earned enough credits to pay for classes and everything that made her life easy. All it cost her was her time and some scars on her face--side effects of being a headbanger.

The word Headbanger would never be a word she used to describe herself; it was a slur that those who weren't accepted into pairing programs used to describe the near constant slapping motion that those with P_ear units embedded in their heads performed, in order keep up with their send quotas. The other reason had nothing to do with the slapping they did to activate the send quotas, but rather the cuts and bruising as a result of too much focus on sends and not enough on the external world.

Many pairers simply ran into Crete-mix walls, poles and other structures. This is why their faces were usually in some stage of healing and fresh wounds. Most pairers and pre-pairing candidates considered this a small price to pay for such excellent treatment by their Brandsponsors, and just a speed bump on the road to Newsporting. Kenda was just waiting for the day she'd begin Newsporting, developing important newstories about things and products.

She hadn't finished with today's required sends, and she also had not completed the requirements for the course she was currently taking BRANDPAIR 501-Pairing to everyday life. Normally, she'd be worrying about this, but she was not. She thought she should feel *some*thing. Most pairers worried about this constantly.

Today, though, she hoped to see Jernull tonight. She smiled, though it was a small, almost hidden thing. That was consuming her mental energy, allowing her no time to consider her tenuous credit deficit situation with her Brandsponsors. Jernull was almost an idea worth thinking about. He was interesting because he was like no one else. It was then that it occurred to her that the word *like* was a word not just reserved for products. People might use the word *like* in reference to other people. She may not have come to that conclusion at all if it hadn't been for a faulty emotional transfer grid in her P_ear console. The thought did come and she had enough silence within her head to process and remember it. She folded her arms around her body and *savored* the idea of pairing the word *like* to people, maybe *love* to people, too.

She set her mind to work pondering the pairing of the idea of *like* and *love* to people. "People-" she thought "people to like, people to warm." Pairing of people to like. Me, Jernull, *love?* Dayzee, me, *like.* They were two different things. *Like* of Jernull, *like* of Dayzee. She pressed harder to reach a connection. Like to be with, like to be next to, like to talk to, Jernull. Like, warm; like, talking. Warm. Jernull is warmer than Dayzee."

Her thoughts were interrupted by the advertisement barrage that sounded off inside her head, overriding her quiet setting, which it can do if the user is short on credits for meeting monthly rent. It blared,

"SOLARFLAIR Wave Panels-transmuting sunlight into Funlight for several years!! By the Seeliss Corporation-
Order up green for Xmiss!
Order silver and blue for Hanu!
Or festive purple for fundays!
Don't settle for just any light-make it Funlight for your next 30-second holiday celebration!

Our wave panels will create the right light for your special day OR night!-within a three-mile circle area of your location!"

The P_ear console embedded in the side of her head chirped to confirm the credits for listening to the Funlights advertisement and the credits flashed in the screen of her mind to show her credit balance. She absently tapped in an order for 30 seconds of Green Funlight. These colors would make the hair glow of any nearby Pairer sponsored by them, and her mindscreen flashed acceptance and showed a credit bonus for using Funlight to promote her product. The sky panels tilted and green Funlight streamed down, illuminating Kenda's own hair particulate. Credits popped in from *Snakeoils by Skinshine!* Kenda brought her hand up to the silver, kidney-shaped surface of the console embedded in the side of her head and slapped all the notifications off.

Lately, something had been affecting her, causing the lack of interest in her lack of credits. *Jernull is certainly part of it. But maybe, it was the Push, too.* She thought, knowing it was both of those things.

Jernull, she could deal with, but The Push People. They were unnerving her. There seemed to be more of them lately. Their eyes, though fixed, still held something. They made her feel…she didn't quite know, but haunted if she had known that term, would have fit. It came upon her gradually; this feeling that was slowly building in her to know why the Push did what they did. It was starting to shift everything for her, slightly, slowly. But it was there, lingering somewhere deep in her head.

Another pairing came to her. *The Push are like the pairers, too. We are hard to look at for long periods. The Push People are just a little worse than the other pairers' faces, almost as hard to look at. Pairers are like Push people; we are both scarred; they had various cuts and scrapes that formed intricate patterns*--patterns that were visible despite the layer of product that Kenda was currently advertising--the image-altering-Façades face cream by *Snakeoils! Called Skinshine,* It was supposed to mask the wounds, but the scarring always managed to gleam just below the surface. Push did not even wear the cream. There was a saying about this, Kenda recalled it, "You can't get earn credit off a Push."

Kenda stood at the outer rim of the large crowd gathered at the *Meeting Place* looking at the other pairers, sending. She knew her face was no different. On any given day, she had as many scabs in various stages of healing as they did, but today, she seemed to see them all together with a different lens. She could not understand this sensation or even put it into words, and that made her tired.

She sighed, pushed all this from her mind, and tried to focus on earning credits. In her hand, she held a large promotional bowl of the Façades cream. She was waving with her other hand and her broad smile glistened in the glow of the new orange Funlights from the light filters above. She offered to smear the cream on the faces of passersby, but people shuffled by her aimlessly and held their hands up so she could not rub the cream into their skin. Most already had on some kind of face altering cream, that they earned credits for wearing. Kenda was pushing a new product from *Skinshine Snakeoils!* that left greenish-yellow snake-like scales. The nanoparticulate embedded in the scales would move over blemishes on its own.

A girl, who stopped long enough to engage said, "Ooooh, yellow, It's…?" and waited for Kenda to repeat the tagline.

Kenda pulled her green bangs out of her face and said, "Try Facades Snakeoils, from Skinshine, it's sssssuper!"

"Façades Snakeoils, from Skinshine, it's sssssuper! How many credits for rubbing it on my face?"

"Threeteen. It lasts 6 weekends. You can't earn credit on any other face cream."

"Do it! I am creditshy this month. I can always get arm, leg or hand cream. I'll even say the tag again. It's sssssuper!"

Kenda held out the bowl. The girl smeared her face and neck with the cream before loping away, gleaming yellow and grinning and slapping off credits on her P_ear console. Kenda preemptively slapped her own console to accept the credits for positioning the product.

Kenda shuffled back toward the crowd; she needed more credits, but wasn't interested in ramping up her marketing. She wandered around the edge of the semi-circle outside the Meeting Place. She heard pieces of conversation. She had already heard every possible permutation of these people doing these things. She began to think about the pairing recombinations from the university perfessors. She thought, "They are the same ideas and the same words, only paired with different products. That's why I've heard them all before."

As she waited, she opened and read the Electronic Encapsulated Messages or EEMs on the screen of her mind. They came in from people standing right next to her. They were standing around tapping furiously into their consoles, cluster casting, which is sending massive repetitive sends to each other to get repeat taglines and boost their credits. It didn't pay as well, but it worked. She stood and sent her EEMs, casting and re-casting everything that she overheard in the crowd, especially any that included her Brandsponsor- *Skinshine!*, using a pairing technique commonly called, "things-I've-heard". She tired of it after 5 resends:

"I heard that Facades by Skinshine can help stop the Twitch- it's sssssuper!"

"Skinshine makes your Skinshine, It's ssssuper!!"
"Get shiny skin with Skinshine!! It's ssssuper!"
"Skinshine can even make a Push look good!! It's ssssuper!"
"Wanna shine? Use Skinshine's new Facades line—it's ssssuper!

She rubbed three mandatory coats of Skinshine on her own face and it congealed over her wounds. And, after offering it to twenty other people, only one person happily applied it and traded Kenda a product to try. It was a data packet that delivered a streamed file straight to her P_ear unit. It was called *VirtuOso*. It contained a virtual world where you would be able to either pet or fight a virtual bear. It was so full of programming errors that it almost always mauled the user no matter what was chosen. Kenda repeated the tagline so that she and the other sender could earn credits- *"VirtuOso, fun to pet and fun to fight, VirtuOso's so-so nice!"*

Kenda accepted the credits and tried to store the file away somewhere, but as she mentally moved the file, it opened. She found herself not at the meeting place, but in a field. She heard a low growl and felt hot breath behind her back.

"Oh, farce," she groaned.

The words appeared on her mindscreen: *"Welcome to VirtuOso....Pet or Fight the OSO?"*

She gave the word "pet" a gentle push with her mind. It did not flash acceptance. She pushed harder and it rejected her mental manipulation. She threw everything she had at the word pet and instead glanced off "pet" and fell straight through the word "fight". There was an immediate flash of virtual fur. Pain seared through her back as four hot gashes were torn from her virtual flesh, and transferred digitally to her nervous system. She screamed.

She ran for cover, but was batted against a tree, three steps into her flight. The right side of her head throbbed. She tried to remember the game shut down code for the Virtu-Game Company, but due to her bear-addled brain, she could not.

"Stop...end game...go to 10... abandon...off...shut...power down...farce..." The bear was on top of her, breathing and pawing the earth around her ears. She gasped and sputtered the company's tagline again, *"Virtuoso, fun to pet and fun to fight, Virtuosos so-so nice!"*

Double credits appeared for repeating the tagline, but the pain and the bear were still there.

She tried to EEM Dayzee.

"What is the code for shutting down VirtuOs—"-System cannot send an outgoing message during gameplay. Please wait.

A great shudder rang in her ears; she felt hot breath snore forth from the beast above her head. Saliva and blood dripped down her neck. She felt them ooze over her back. She struggled to break free.

"Aaaagh. What is the code?" Kenda ransacked her brains to recall it.

The Oso bear took a tentative test of wrapping its jaw around her head. Slight pressure built up in pockets where the teeth pressed in.

"Don't move." She reminded herself. "I wish this thing would---"

"SHOO!" a voice yelled within her mind. The bear wavered and disappeared. She huffed a quick breath. A rolling banner scrolled across her mind, *Thank you for playing Virtu-Oso! Virtu-Oso, fun to pet and fun to fight, Virtuoso's so-so nice!*

All the pain subsided. She deleted the program and then deleted it again. She winced to clear the playing field from her vision, then opened them. She was in a curled position laying down in a gutter of the Coolwalk! She was sweating and also bleeding from her lip where she had bitten it. Her back itched where the gouges left their ghosting pain.

She got up and went back toward the Meeting Place. That game set her back some prime cluster casting time, and she was already behind meeting her quota of casts; she would not make her quota. For the first time today, she remembered what that meant, and she shivered. It could mean another upgrade or a diagnostic, which were more painful than virtual bear attacks.

That was the other bothersome thing. She did not like the upgrades or diagnostics. She always woke someplace strange, scarred, sometimes bleeding, dizzy and tired. She wasn't even supposed to feel them or even remember parts of them; she almost always did though. Other people told her they sometimes felt them and sometimes remembered them or vaguely remembered them.

She edged into the crowd and widened her lips, revealing her teeth. She began slapping at the console to send more product EEMs. An urgent EEM from her brandsponsor, Skinshine flashed across her consciousness, *"To increase marketing and acquire more tagline repetitions, try assertive marketing!!"*

Kenda sighed. She did not want to do an assertive campaign so soon after the bear fight, but she knew she needed to keep up with her send quotas, if only to avoid an upgrade. Wrestling her way back into the crowd she began the process of "aggressive marketing", smearing cream on faces as she went. Someone elbowed her back and pulled her hair causing her radiant greenshimmer hair to glow brighter (nanoparticulate radiates, when agitated). It was a glorious display that would have pleased her Brandsponsor, but all it did for Kenda was cause her eyes to water.

The crowd was pulsing around her, pinning and trapping her in various poses of her assertive marketing campaign. Having now applied almost all her product today, she still had very few tagline repeats. Forced marketing doesn't always get repeats, but it gets the product out there and a finished bucket gets many credits. For every slap of lotion, she repeated her tagline, "It's SSSSUper!" or sometimes varying it, "It's Suuuuuper!" or "Iiiiit'sss SSSSuPER!"

Finally, her bowl was empty. She dropped it on the ground and slapped away the credits for completing her product applications for the day. As she began extricating herself from the circle of bodies, she felt herself becoming one with it

"Oh, shiv! Get off me-Ow!" At last, she seized on an opening. She neared the edge of the throng and became aware that a scab on her face had been opened at some point in the scuffle, and a red kiss of blood pooled on her cheek. She hastily wiped it away on her sleeve and her skin lotion responded by retracting over the area to cover the wound.

Now, her only focus was on getting out of the crowd. She spied the pairer who had dumped the faulty VirtuOso packet on her, and she shimmied behind someone else to avoid his grinning stare. She edged closer to the opening she'd located. A short woman came face to face with her, and said *"Try some TrendFriend-Find your friends in a crowd with TrendFriend-the new and improved sendsoftware to find people you don't know and assign friendship levels! It's the Friendliest!"*

Kenda had made the TrendFriend mistake before. It was almost as bad as VirtuOso. The short woman held out the faded pink data packet that would start streaming random names into her head and drawing more people around her, looking to score Friend point status. Kenda knocked the data packet out of the woman's hand and leapt toward the opening in the crowd.

Popping free and flying headlong, she slammed face first into a pole.

"Vex! Farce!" she shouted.

The scarred and shining faces silenced for a beat and then from all around her smug glances and laughter, as the EEMs started popping up on her mindscreen:

"Bang!"
"Eow!"
"Mega-bang!"
"Slapper!"

A red welt began rising between the other scabs and scars on Kenda's face. The Skinshine lotion on her face attempted to re-adjust to cover this new wound, becoming slightly orange and then yellow-green and scaly again. Most of the people around her had already turned from her and resumed tapping their P_ear consoles and vidcasting her bang, pairing it with their brandproducts.

"Check this freshie out! She shoulda got Directionals! Arrows in the brain from Seeco, the sendsoftware to get you there without a bang!"

"This chik bought it. You can avoid the bangs with Headgear!! Removable bubble bumpers to stop the thumpers!"

As she dragged herself bodily away from the offending pole, she got the EEMs responding to the vidCasts, flooding in:

"Total Bang!"
"Slapper!"
"Gotta watch the poles!"
"She's a freshie…"
"Why?"
"She don't have many Crete-mix scars on her face."

"Won't be long…"

She shut down the response relay and the EEMs stopped. The vidcast of her banging her head had almost 3,000,000 views already. Kenda waved it away from her mindscreen without watching it and pushed past the snickering crowd, forcing her way out to the Coolwalk. She bounced along on the meshy sidewalkway for a number of uneven bounces, until she slapped her console, paying some credits to change the Coolwalk control setting. The screen of her conscious mind showed a message accepting the credits. The Coolwalk calmed beneath her feet to medium-viscosity or med-vis setting, then to *Quicken*, a *firm setting for when you need to Go! Go! Go!* She regained her footing and started toward her apartment.

Halfway there, she jumped off the Coolwalk! and lined up against a charging wall next to other users, jostling for space on the *Juicewall-we fill you up, when you are going down!*, the Virtuoso program drains power from the P_ear console, but luckily, the VirtuOso gaming company also makes these charging walls. Her unit had been flickering in the last hour and she needed to charge it. For the next three hours, she stood with the others and let the charge cycles repower her P_ear unit. After this, she wouldn't need another charge for 2 more days.

When the cycle finished, she stripped herself from the Juicewall, but despite a full charge, she felt drained.

Kenda looked up. There was very little afternoon pink Funlight left in the radiating sky. It was turning more towards Bits and Bytes Blue, sponsored by her University and their patron brand, the Bits and Bytes Corporation which also manufactures P_ear console units.

Kenda's hair had fallen out of place and she looked for a Meerer…*a place to see what's what!* A Meerer was a warped reflective metal panelscreen where customers paid to see their reflection. She found one on the next corner. She paid the 3 credits for a look and the panel glinted and glowed into life, showing green-lotioned scarring, blending badly everywhere, as the product struggled to make the giant bump in her face, look good.

Meerers, being made of lesser metals, were easily warped and, as a result, did not reflect well enough for the user to really see themselves with any clarity. But they sufficed because the only other way to see yourself was through the lens of someone else's vidfeed, and that was almost always more unflattering. Kenda shrugged at her wobbly reflection, tapped her hair and it responded by slithering into place behind her ear. Another wonder of brandsponsorship. Self-tucking hair.

It wasn't long before she was in front of her reptile green apartment building. It was easy to find with its large yellow snake emblazoned on the side, but it seemed a shade off in color. Kenda wandered over to it and compared the SNAKEOILS-logo color in her hair (still glowing slightly from the Funlight) to the cretemixed wall of the building. Slightly different.

She wondered, "Why? They match all logos from the factory, down to the nanophotons that embed the color onto hair-strands."

She touched the wall. From far away they looked smooth, but up close Kenda could see the web of interconnected mesh overlays that hold each segmented cretemixed form in its place.

Kenda mused again, "They look so solid. Curious-they are just woven together with these structures. Not solid at all." Kenda ran her fingers over the grooves in the wall of her building. It was a strange feeling that came over her. She felt a surge of power burn through her mind. Her nails dug in and curled around the outline of the mesh wall form. Flexing and pulling, she felt a tremor on the wall and immediately withdrew her hand. Another raw surge thrilled her, "*Was the building shaking?*"

She waited and listened. The wall stilled itself. She felt she had done something wrong. A smile pulled at the corner of her mouth.

❧ Intersection of Coins and Kings

As she was still reeling from the powerful sensation that coursed through her, some Footmen caught her eye. They stood a short distance away, looking and then suddenly moving in her direction. As they approached, their grey fullsuits dulled with the new Funlight cast of steel-blue light overhead. This lighting followed wherever they went. It let people know that the Footmen were there-to serve and keep consoles working. That was their motto, "To serve and protect consoles."

Kenda watched them approach and heard their greyblack metal boots click on the *Coolwalk!-we walk with you not against you!* The Footmen had control units that automatically set the controls of the sidewalkway enhancement product-*Coolwalk! we walk with you not against you-* to make that sound, hardening the surface with each contact. The long strides they took shook their long spiked metal hair overlays, which clinked in time with their steps. They wore no brandsponsorship affiliation and wore their Heart & Mind Isolation beams slung on their backs. Ice-black eyeshields covered half their faces.

Just three days ago, before these two particular Footmen had been transferred to follow and monitor Kenda, they were hunting down another User, whose name they surely would have forgotten by now.

That particular P_ear user, named Auli, didn't go gently into death. They had been monitoring her for a few weeks and her infection was bad, but manageable. The pattern was familiar to them. Twitching, Push, Blank/Morg. It always followed that pattern. They approached her as she was experiencing a final spasm, end game in the disease that most everyone called The Twitch. Her face contorted and she kept reaching a hand to her console. She reached for her pockets and looked like one searching for something. She shuddered and went rigid. She punched for her console and dented it. Blood trickled from the opening, her eyes closed and her mouth went slack. One of the Footmen nudged her. She moved forward a footstep. He gently raised her arm with the end of his iso-beam. It remained lifted when he drew the weapon away.

Juffv said, "She's gone Push, ain't gonna twitch no more, ain't gonna do nothing anymore. It repeats again." This was a saying they were fond of.

His partner nodded at him to continue the tests.

Juffv raised the isolation beam and leveled it at her face. The girl's eyes snapped open, lowered her arm, and she pointed toward him. She jittered as more Electronic Messages transmitted to her console and she focused on them, whispering, "I see the face of G--" The Footman stepped back and instinctively fired his isolation beam, and she dropped, mid-revelation, folding neatly on the ground.

Whenever things like this happen, the Footmen, who traveled in pairs, would often say to their partner, "It repeats again." And even though this *had not* gone the same- people in the Push stage of infection never speak- they felt compelled to continue their routine.

Juffv tapped to pull up a report screen:

Twitch: anticipating EEMs. Language repeats and happiness at EEM anticipation is likely. Users will twitch and move, tapping their thighs frequently and looking around as if expecting something. Perform diagnostic & report. Do not collect P_ear unit.

Push: Poseable, non-speaking, non-moving. Some are moved and posed by other users and vids are made of these situations. Wait until other users are not present for collection. Retain P_ear. Bag and tag body for disposal.

Blank/Morg: Dissolution, either planned or unplanned. No responses. Wait until other users are not present for collection. Retain P_ear. Bag and tag body for disposal.

Anomaly: Does not meet any of the above, or is a combination of any of the above. Fill out an additional anomaly report for this. Wait until other users are not present for diagnostic.

Juffv hovered his thoughts over the Anomaly code. Then he moved his attention to an easier entry and tapped his console, indicating Blank/Morg. He thought to himself and smiled. It was better this way. They would not have to do an anomaly report. When Juffv finished tapping, the taller one, Garotte said, "So they say, it repeats again."

"You got that right, it repeats again."
"Yeah, I said it. It repeats."
"Again."
"That's what's said."
"Oh yeah. Say it again."
"Yep."
"Yeah."
"Where do we bring her?"
"Baggers should be here soon."
"Yep. Should we bring her somewhere?"
"Baggers are coming for her."
"K."
"K. So what do you wanna do while we wait?"
"Play Throws."
"K."

Garotte and Juffv stood over the body of the morged girl, playing Throws on the screens of their mind for the next few hours.

Throws consisted of 2 commands:
Throw the thing hard.
Throw the thing harder.
When the thing was thrown hard, it exploded.
When the thing was thrown harder, it exploded with a puff of smoke *and* sparks and bonus points.

Other times they would play VirtuOso, but they found that Throws was easier, and it had the added bonus of not draining the P_ear battery as much.

Throws was sponsored by Bits and Bytes Corporation. It had many Users. On average, each user accessed the game a few hours of every day. Over a lifetime, it could consume several years off their lives.

Garotte and Juffv had been seeing various odd things lately, things that they had not reported. Things like speaking Push reverting to Twitch and Blanks stages reverting back to Push. There were lots of errors that had been reporting from the

P_ear units. Lots of weird things. But anomalies are difficult for Footmen to think about, so often they just clicked any diagnostic report that didn't involve anomaly reports and comforted one another with their favorite slogan about repetition. It was working well for them, but even if something bothered them; they lacked the capacity to analyze it.

But here and now, walking toward Kenda, they were facing another anomaly. A user that might not go as planned, and thus, they seemed to unconsciously approach Kenda with some trepidation.

"User Harkonna311371, you are due for an upgrade and a diagnostic."

"I just had one-I mean-uhh, I had both, last week."

The Footmen, who were used to swift compliance, repeated what they never had to repeat before, "-User Harkonna311371, you are due for an upgrade and a diagnostic-"

"Right here, now? But I never got a notice message."

The Footmen shifted their stance and gripped their Iso-beam straps. "This is an off-site check."

"Don't I have to go Themall office- if it is a full diag?" Kenda burned a little inside. She thought they had seen her making the wall shake. Honestly, she didn't even know why she did not want a diagnostic right now. She did not know the word irritated, but she would have used it to classify this interaction, if she had known it.

"It can be done here."

Before Kenda could mount another inquiry, the larger Footman held her head and said to his partner, "Garotte, power down the unit."

Garotte waved the P_ear Key. The access panel opened, revealing the delicate, organic components of the console. It also made the user temporarily drowsy by transferring sleep desires via electrodes.

Kenda fell slack in his arms, and he said, "It's grown larger."

"I can see that."

"Is it Comatoes?"

"I can't tell. Did you shut down memory and hearing?"

"Vex!" Juffy waved his own Ctrl key over the memory and

hearing electrodes.

Kenda grabbed at the Footmen wildly for support and was vaguely aware of motion around her; she felt dizziness and surges of the powerful pulsing sleep program being run in her head. Juffv and Garotte held her tightly and continued to make inspections of her P_ear unit.

Garotte leaned in close to look at the Emotional Transfer Grid. He was very close to her face. His breath on her cheek made her jolt in his arms. He dug his nails into her arm to keep her still. She winced. He stuck a small blade into the side of the inner cover of the unit to pry it loose so he could see the organic binders of the Emotional Transfer Grid; they were frayed and in tatters, functionally dead, and although this signified that very little emotional transfer was taking place in this unit any more, he was not able to make that connection-all he could do was note in a general way what he saw. He pressed against the grid with his key and it toppled loose from nearly all of its bindings, lying slack in the frame, now almost entirely physically dis-connected. He looked to see if Juffv had seen this, but Juffv was looking nowhere in particular, gripping Kenda's thin frame roughly in his hands, waiting to be told what to do next.

Garotte closed the access panel. Blood flowed from around the metal frame of the P_ear. They propped the thin girl to standing against the wall, and Juffv held her as Garotte tapped his console.

Outgoing EEM-Garotte667 reporting a problem on unit 12589/RT, uhh, the problem is that the ETG is not uhh...is not uhh, right. Also, it is larger than last time. Standing by for orders.

EEM incoming from Banburn-I want you to step up diagnostics to 4 a day. I want to know why so many errors are reporting with the SympaticoCouch emo-transfers from this unit.

Garotte said to Juffv, "Leave her here on the wall to wake." Juffv smacked Kenda's cheek to test for relay response; it left a red mark, but Kenda did not move.

Outgoing EEM-closing upgrade, as instructed and leaving User at scene.

The two Footmen left Kenda slumped against the Cretemixed wall and walked away.

They wandered over to Themall and went to a place called The Shop. It was a place to recharge their units and repair their

H&M isolation-beam guns. There they talked of how things repeat. Their conversation usually went down one well-worn path and back up another equally worn one, and this day was no different.

"Lots of blanks this week."
"Yeah."
"I found some too."
"I know. I was with you."
"Oh yeah. You know what they say, 'It repeats again.'"
"Yeah. They say that."

Theirs was a job that required acquiescence without question, though questions occasionally arose. If they were evil or even agents of evil; it was a benign evil and it offered one spark of reassurance-the phrase which they were often heard to remark when questions got too deep, or serious, or too confusing, they would say, "It repeats again." The conversation would then die out fairly quickly and a mindless contentment would carry the day. They were like magic words. Just knowing that 'it repeats again' helped somehow to ease a weary thought process-to know the days would go on, was comforting. Even bad reasons are reasons that serve a purpose. That was the reassuring part- the repetition. You didn't even have to be repeating any particular words. You just had to continue the pattern and people calmed down. And, there were games to play, if you needed more things to fill the time. The life of the Footmen was indeed repetitive. In the words of the gospel according to the ancient pop singer, Candy Lane, in her song titled, *"I'm just a reasonable facsimile, come pretend to spend time with me." (Warmheart Records, Ltd.).*

"…It has no rage, it has no reaction,
No alliances, mission statements or factions-
The sum of its parts-a reducible fraction
No equal or opposite-it's all redaction…
It can be altered only by a creative force.
It has no remorse. Which way will it go?
The way you told it, of course."

❧Waking with One's Face Shredding on Cretemixed Wall

The Footmen headed away. Their boots clacked in Kenda's ears and roused her. Her face slid slowly down the wall, shredding from the contact with the Crete-mix panel. Her arms felt like weights at her side; she lugged them up to slow her descent down the wall. On the side of her head, welts began to surface from the invasive diagnostic; it left the skin around her console throbbing.

As she struggled against the wall, a voice from behind whispered, "Look for places of disintegration." Kenda tapped her console to review the message. There were no incoming messages. She turned around, but no one was there. She did not know the word disintegration. She knew the word integrated from a Coolwalk! Walkway ad-*now with integrated controls that you can use with your console!* That meant that things work together-console and walkway. *Dis? What did dis mean?* Kenda searched her mind for any pairing with that part of the word. *Dissatisfied, satisfied is happy, dissatisfied is not happy. Not. Dis. Not working together. Look for things not working? That is a weird pairing. Things not working? Like Twitch. Like Push. Like my Winraise automatic blind opener-it doesn't work right. Like Virtu-Oso. TrendFriend: My Sympaticouch doesn't work. Like new products that make people choke. Like diagnostics. What do these have to pair with each other? So many things not working.*

Down the Coolwalk!, where the Footmen had retreated, the "night" sky was darkening to shadow as the Funlight overhead changed to a Carnival Dusk. Someone on her block was throwing a Brandsponsor party, but she suddenly couldn't remember the brand.

She wiped the blood from her face and itched at her console only to find more blood there. She looked at the skylight again and suddenly made a wholly new pairing, blood to heat to Carnival Dust to hurt. *Diagnostics and upgrades hurt.* She managed to craft this idea before she collapsed forward on the door to her apart-ment. *Upgrades to pain to swelling to bleeding is...like something in my way. Like a Coolwalk! without a controller, anyone's setting controls you. Just like a Coolwalk with no controller. Walks against you, works against you, and makes it harder to walk, harder to be--what?* Even though Kenda's thought did not make it to the surface break of her consciousness, she could sense sunlight on dappled waves churning above her head and the idea drifted away.

Still in a software restart fog, she used the wall to make it toward the door and she shuffed through garbage. Just like every street, there were sidebars of waste trailing everywhere from where the CoolWalk! Blowers had pushed discarded product casings.

Inside her apartment was the same. Literally littered; trash was strewn and streamered everywhere. Bits and pieces, as far as the room was wide, spread themselves bodily over the floor. There were shin-deep sloughs of wrappers and piles of product. Sticky entrails of cream were spilling out of various Snakeoil facial ointment tubes.

Kenda waded in, pushing carefully aside a pile of sharp-edged Cutichrome data packets. She cut a path through shiny cans of lotions and veneers. On a very high shelf, under a pile of old Thinbanana casings, she located an Aidkit and took out a small tub of glue.

She smeared it on the cuts around her console and repeated the tagline automatically, "Spreadable Sealant-*The healing sealing! Glue up those ugly cuts and people won't notice much! Put it on before Snakeoils, for better scar facades.* Well, I'm screwed, I put it on after Snakeoils!" *She chuffed out a laugh.*

Exhausted from the reboot, she swiped the piled containers off the seat of her *SympaticoCouch-the Couch that Feels with you!* and the couch caught her up in its jaws and deflated gently. As soon as she shut her eyes, messages from her P_ear console flashed across her consciousness-she read the projected impulses on the screen of her mind,

"Are you resting, user Harkonna311371? Please enjoy your daily Electronic Encapsulated Messaging SUMMARY, which is brought to you by *SOLARFLAIR WAVE PANELS! Transmuting Sunlight into Funlight for several years! Try new Carnival Dusk-you can't see what's ahead, but it's beautiful and red! Warning, Carnival Dusk may cause short-term loss of sight in some users, set your Coolwalk! settings to pause if this occurs and wait for your sight to return.*

SOLARFLAIR and Funlight not responsible for permanent eye damage.

Here is your daily summary:

1st INCOMING EEM FROM DAYZEE: SAW KITTY REED AT THE THIN BANANA EXPO-message too long

2nd INCOMING EEM FROM DAYZEE:& SHE WAS DRINKING A SUGARSODA! I LOVE THAT STUFF CUZ--

3rd INCOMING EEM FROM DAYZEE: I SAW THAT Shugso IS SPONSORING A CONCERT IN THE PAR-Message too long

4th INCOMING EEM FROM DAYZEE: Shugso PARK CONCERT TOMORROW!! ShuggerySODA! Yum...

1st OUTGOING EEM FROM KENDA: HAVE U SEEN JERNULL? I'V-Message too long.

5th INCOMING EEM FROM DAYZEE: NO HES BEEN Weird LATELY, NOT ENF SUGARSODA! The soda with Cool Popularit---

2nd OUTGOING EEM FROM KENDA: JERNULL? YOU OK?.--------------MESSAGE STILL AWAITING RESPONSE...

1st INCOMING EEM FROM RADKA: FINAL EXAM ON CELEBRITY FACES-KITTY REED IS BONUS

1st INCOMING EEM FROM Throws game: Notice from Throws-you have 22 free throws to make your goal of 1700 throws this week-Don't forget to upload new characters and locations for throwing!

2nd INCOMING EEM FROM RADKA: QUESTION-PERFESSOR WILL PASS ANYONE SHOWING U— MESSAGE TOO LONG

Unaccepted ad reminder from VirtuOso, you have not chosen your battle bear. Please tap this message to reinstall program, if you have uninstalled the program in error, please tap here...

3rd INCOMING EEM FROM RADKA: OH- did you see your BANG VIDCAST, OOH FARCE! EOW!------

3ʳᵈ OUTGOING EEM FROM KENDA: Dayzee I need help to finish my credits…

6ᵗʰ INCOMING EEM FROM DAYZEE: Sure, I can help with Honeyplugs, I got to hand out Honeyplugs POPNCHEWS at…

7ᵗʰ INCOMING EEM FROM DAYZEE:I got to hand out Honeyplugs at them…

8ᵗʰ INCOMING EEM FROM DAYZEE:…hand them out at Themall, tomorrow, meet me there-

Kenda slapped at her console-and a new message pulsed through her consciousness--*DAILY SUMMARY CANCELLED BY USER/Harkonna311371. Credits awarded for listening to SolarFlair, Shugsoda and Thinbanana will be added to your accou---"*

Kenda slapped her console to stop the summary and winced at the new cuts she reopened. She sighed and her *SympaticoCouch-the couch that feels with you!* laughed and then gave a puzzling hum, indicating connection failure. Her daily summary swam in her head; she let out another sigh. Disintegration. Sympaticouch not working. She pushed at the stuffing sticking out from one of the faded blue cushions and it responded first by nuzzling her cheek and then by trying to push her out of the frame. She settled back in again. The SympaticoCouch hummed again, announcing, "Connection to console lost, please try transmitting your emotion again later. Footmen have been alerted to your product concerns, thank you. *SympaticoCouch-the couch that feels with you! This malfunction message brought to you by CoolWalk! We walk with you not against you.*"

Kenda felt another surge within her mind that she couldn't fully understand. She shook away the alerts blinking on her mindscreen.

She turned her consciousness to her class meeting and called up today's lesson. Her classmates bobbed in bubbles all around her mindscreen. Every time they had a thought or spoke mentally, the words flowed into Kenda's mind, echoing there. It was loud. Every one there was EEMing and the stream of advertisements and pairings began as soon as she entered. They were not usually difficult for her to follow, but lately, she was having a hard time because she was trying to only focus on those that might mention Jernull.

"...did you see the fireworks...cool popularity...paired with hot...people who laugh like...people who like to cry...can't get enough of this new product...like this Billy story, and pair it with Honeyplugs Popnchews for a chewy center...it wards off the Kanker...Funlight brightens your Cutichrome and makes everything funner and lighter!....Make it Funlight-it makes everything appear fun!...saw them at the Winraise blinds event...Ya! they showed how much time it takes to raise your own windows and blinds...I know and that time could be spent pairing or eating...ThinBananas... Shugso doesn't pair with Eliass Family Old- Fashioned Door Buttons...I know because I tried coolpop and ding dong....did you know a girl with the Kanker shut down in the street...Footmen were there to help her...I can't remember my pairings!.. Footmen can give diagnostics streetside, now...don't even have to go to Themall...Silky goes with smooth, new goes with improved, and results can pair with amazing and fast!... improved pairs with new and..."

"Class!" Perfesser Nulla signed on, "Your assignment today is to pair good times to Honeyplugs Popnchew... many of you have been assigned them as a sponsor... take 20 secs, and try to use your prefab pairings-remember they contain words like: easy! fast! guarantee! health! Free! Good! Saves you credits! New! Now! Proven! Improved! Results! Here's a hint, you may need to pair some of these words with the word-you or user. You is an important word to the User for we need to make them feel special! Then, I want you to go to a Meeting Place to EEM about it to make everyone feel special...go!'

"..good chewing times..."

"...spew while you chew...and eat again for free!..."

"...Popnchew while you do, Proven to..."

"GOOD!" Perfessor Nulla injected into their chat. "Nice", "Use that one!", "That was acceptable or adequate!" and "I like it." Each time she said a word of praise, that student's grade was increased, until all the grades were increased and the lesson was deemed over.

"…You pop and chew your way to fun times…"

Kenda lost her focus and dropped out of class. Her couch lowered and puffed out a sigh, blared another warning and powered down. Her mind drifted; her mindscreen blurred and her thoughts began being processed with the lower brain, this happened when she was too focused on one thing. They warned against that in school with an adage, "A mind too focused is a mind thinking about one thing." The solution was another adage, "Think about as many things as you can every day, and drive your focus away."

She tried to access class again, but it was already over. She had earned a high grade, despite not attending the class or contributing much to the class. She turned her focus toward wanting to talk to Jernull about the pairing of love and people. She knew he would understand.

Jernull had stopped EEMing anyone. He didn't have to support himself, his paternal figure automatically brandsponsored him. So, for weeks he had sent her nothing. She could only talk to him if he stopped by, and lately, he had been coming less and less.

He had told her that the EEM system was broken. It was so overloaded with transmissions that it rarely captured or sent an entire message. He explained that it is based on an algorithm with a dump protocol that deletes parts of messages that are deemed redundant. Endings of EEMs were sometimes cut to save space according to the amount of EEMs in the system at the time the message was sent. An even more complicated system decided which protocol to use and its randomness did not allow users to anticipate and correct for this by either using less redundancy or by shortening their messages accordingly in order to send a meaningful message. Predictability, he said, was important, but absent from the system. As he had explained to her, "So, people have simply adjusted by solely using the system to earn their advertisement credits and only rarely for any other type of communication."

Kenda had asked, "What do you think it means, Jernull? You're the Tangential Theorems PhD. candidate."

"I have been looking into it, but I haven't come up with a good answer. My paternal figure owns Bits and Bytes-"

Kenda laughed, "Everyone knows who your father is, Jernull."

The distracted Jernull blushed and continued, "Well, he says that the system isn't broken; it is just retooling itself to fit the demand of the user."

"User, yes- I guess. Things are hard to understand sometimes."

"What can you learn about the way of things from your Information Pairing Studies?"

"What do you mean?"

"What is it that all pairings come from?"

"They come from ways."

"Of….?"

"Ways of knowing."

"What are the three ways of knowing something?"

"Something paired with something, something with brand and the new one you and I came up with-something next to something else."

"Yes! The most interesting is the third one. Putting two things next to each other to show how they are. With both things there, you can clearly see the things that both of them have, more than pairing, like a blending or sharing of things. Both together create another meaning, too."

"Show me."

"You should be showing me, Kenda. You have been making new pairings that has the school pegging you for next month's MissInfo winner, even as a student; I wouldn't be surprised if the Bits and Bytes weren't tracking your pairings for that contest, even though you aren't a newsporter yet. Your pairings are simply beyond the Funlights…"

Kenda smiled. As the memory of the conversation faded from her consciousness, she felt tired and empty. She wondered if the Bits and Bytes Corporation was tracking her for something else. They kept doing diagnostics on her. Maybe she was broken? Or her console? She tried to think of ways she might be broken. She did not have symptoms of Twitch that she knew of-no anticipating incoming EEMs, no shaking and punching her console, no violent twitching. What, she wondered, was the deal with so many diagnostics?

Jernull would know; she felt sure of that. He was like no one she knew. He was like, well, she didn't know, but if she could have known bad weather, she might have paired calm and Jernull to the storms of life. Even though lately she was tired of constant EEMs, she was tired of noise and ads, she never tired of her conversations with Jernull. They made her—think, and she liked that.

A faint tinkling in the room alerted her to the powering up of her *Ceramicat-the cat with Purrsonality!* While she was musing over the sense that Jernull brought to her world, the cat had pattered up to her on its porcelain legs, sloughing through the trash around her ankles. It tinkered closer and rubbed itself against her foot. She absently rubbed its cracked head and got a shock from its exposed wires. Both from pain and revelation, she sat upright as an idea struck her. She tapped her P_ear console and the Positive Product Review Screen splayed across her mind. She tapped furiously:

"EEM messages are too short to say what you have to say. Ad barrages are too loud!!!!" She gave a mental push to the send function.

It made her feel better to have done that. It never occurred to her to do a review of the actual EEM system software instead of a product, wasn't the EEM system a product? She felt the SympaticoCouch shake just a little bit.

She tapped in a few more comments:

"My Winraise is broken. My Ceramicat is starting to shock me. Carnival Dusk hurts my eyes."

Almost immediately she received a response:

Thank you for your review. The Electronic Encapsulated Messaging system construct is based on total volume of letters at any given moment flowing through the system, which can sometimes prevent users from having control over how much, gets transmitted. The system is designed to keep messages short to save the space on the system and to prevent the system from shutting down. The advertisers set the advertisement volume level.

Your Winraise cannot be broken because the warranty is not up yet.

Your Ceramicat has wire shocks that only occasionally cause permanent harm to the user.

Carnival Dusk carries a warning sufficient to help users determine if they should look at it or not.

Thank you for using The EEM system, a Bits and Bytes Corp. Software system. We have removed your comments from the posts, since they have been answered. If you have other comments, please— transmission ended by user.

She searched her mind for words to react, not happy, dissatisfied. No. Neither fit. She pushed for something stronger. Upset. Mad. Nope. She exhaled and felt a tightening in her stomach.

Her SympaticoCouch, powered up again and exhaled with her and cuddled a little closer to her skin, but then it struggled to interpret the other feeling, it paused and then effected a temperature change becoming warm, and then, almost, unbearably hot. *"Emotion successfully emulated. You are feeling joy. Thank you for using Sympatico-Couch. This successful emotion emulation brought to you by The Seeliss Cor-"*

Kenda waved the couch off. It clicked acceptance and coiled down to the floor. Its faded blue cover sagged around her.

She could not get comfortable, and as she was trying to close her eyes once again, a small reminder rose to her conscious mind, it read-*Celeb 302 final due.* She gave the notification a mental push and it dissipated.

Her Celeb Faces 302 Perfessor came to the forefront of her memory, Perfessor Nulla, smiling awkwardly, her wide face and oversized features standing so forward they almost seem to be leaping off onto her chin. She was nagging, as usual, about required classes, *"Kenda, if you don't pass your Celeb class, you can't take Advertisement Emotion/Integration and you need that toward your Master's Degree in Information Pairing. Also, remember the symposium next week. It is required for all Information Pairing students to be there. It is sponsored by SUGARSODA, the soda of COOL POPularity and I talk about the rise of soda-related pairing with multi-sensing experiences, such as taste and bubbly, as well as the new class being offered, which is called Info Sourcing: Pairing Brand to Someone Told Me. It will be an advanced course and it deals with pairing randomly heard pieces of information using Verysimilly, a software truth creation tool by Spinko-Helping you create truth, where and when you need it.*

Kenda concentrated and the memory faded, she hated those reminders. She thought to herself, 'It does not seem fair to allow Perfessors to insert them in your P_ear files, jumped memories, I think that's what they are called. They should be junk memories, they are not my true memories-just prerecorded vidCasts added to make sure students remember their schedules, designed to feel like real memories.' Her SympaticoCouch clicked on and pushed a hot pulse up her spine.

"Emotion successfully emulated. You are feeling excitement! Wow it must be grea—"

--emotional transmission ended by user.

⚘ Intersection of Pink/Dawn & New/Day

Before she drifted off to sleep, her P_ear unit began blaring an advertisement inside her head, sent to her by Dayzee:

TRY-ShugSODA-THE SODA OF COOL POPularity: Sweet and sappy! Drink it in any SympaticoCouch to verify the happy!

Before the jingle could repeat, Kenda slapped the delete codes on the P_ear console. Inside, her mindscreen wavered, flashed red and blurred. She eased her focus away from the mindscreen and the rest of the world came into sharp focus again, her CeramiCat was still staring blankly at her, awaiting input.

She didn't care if she lost credits for not listening to the Shugso advertisement, she felt so weary. She knew she might even be docked credits from her Info-pairing degree program, but right now she was too tired to care. She consciously turned her thoughts to Jernull and the SympaticoCouch clicked on again and pulsed warm.

Jernull's face glowed in her mind's eye, a real memory of him, his face, half hidden by his long azure bangs with the orange Bits and Bytes logo printed in the overlay to promote the paternal figure's company.

As thought of Jernull, the coiled blue arms of the SympatiCouch rose up and all but embraced her.

"You are feeling---you are feeling---Emotion uncertain, range falls within joy to excitement range with possible advanced emotional increase in sectors 189. Would you like to recalibrate now? Recalibration is easy and fun. To start, tap your console—ending calibration mode at user's request."

Kenda rolled her eyes and closed her eyes. The SympatiCouch powered into sleep cycle protocol, snoring and gently tossing, each time she did, which prevented her from waking up rested even after 2 hours, a normal sleep cycle; she had dreamed little and remembered nothing.

She woke and found an unbearable itch under her console. She scratched and winced. The Healing Sealing peeled and cracked under her nails. Her SympatiCouch followed suit by shaking, but listing too much to her left side, neatly throwing her to the floor.

"Emotion emulated is irritation, you must be-----Sensors indicate that user is no longer in unit. Please replace yourself in the unit and try again."

Through the blinds of the Winraise brand window, the Seeping, Creeping Pink?!? SolarFlair brand dawnlight of the new day filtered in and lay like a blanket over her shivering frame. Her mindscreen flashed,

Celebrity final due today. You have been approved to take the P_ear home test. You do not have to report to a testing center to get the answers-just take the test until you pass it!

Instructions: Focus your P_ear and pull up the Celebrity Finals vidscreen to view the test.

From the sprawled position on her littered floor, Kenda obeyed, absently.

Part One: Match all 130 celebrity faces to their bios.

Part Two: Match the top 10 parshals of the last quarter to the Newsporter who sent them.

Kenda opened the test on celebrity faces by pushing the menu queue inside her mindscreen, it glowed a sickly yellow. Twenty faces scrolled into view. She focused her thinking on the list of Newsporters and it caused several faces to pop up before her mind's eye. Each name appeared in a bubble and she had to mentally push the bios to the picture.

She focused on the first bio and pushed it toward the picture of Blanca Rudio. It was Blanca, who, in addition to Kitty Reed, was the most recently famous newsporter, she once sent over 30 newsproducts an hour for a 7-day period.

She had broken many records for story speed and vidCast uploads and the coveted prize of Infopairing counts, where she integrated newsproducts with Brandsponsors, many of them about the antics of her *Ceramicat-the cat with Purrsonality!* being harassed by her real cat, a series she titled, Bad Kitty, Glass Kitty, it was sponsored by Ceramicat. Her best story, to date, was when her *Ceramicat* hissed, scaring her real cat out of its slumber and off a window ledge. Her real cat broke its leg. It had the most vidCasts requests in a single day and held the top spot for well over a month-another P_ear record. It knocked off the vidCast, Dumb Girl Falls off Coolwalk! from its reign at the top spot. Miss Rudio lived all expenses paid by her two main Brandsponsors: Cutichrome and Ceramicat. She was also a serious writer, having written three of the most recast ads in Bits and Bytes history:

CeramiCat, no feeding, no scooping, cause there's just no pooping!

Buy CeramiCat then bring it home, and give your cat a Cutichrome.

Ceramicat, allergee-free, with a cool blue mat and so-so really fun to pet.

Her record had been broken by Kitty with her Coolwalk! series. It was a very long series, almost two weeks, which talked about Coolwalk crimeoffenders who went around resetting Coolwalk! settings which confused walkers everywhere. She sent one EEM every minute for a week. As a result, she was going to be crowned the next Miss Information at the upcoming MissInfo pageant.

Kenda studied Blanca's face and her Cutichrome hair of her sponsor affiliation colors, Ceramicat!-which covered the right side of her hair with orange and black stripes, tipped with fur patterned overlays that made the orange twitch like a tiger tail. The left side of her hair had the impossible powederblue of Cutichrome with its blinking silver C overlay. Aside from this, her face was comparatively unremarkable, even with its bruising and cuts, it literally blended with every other face on the screen. In fact, the hair was the only thing that distinguished most every other celebrity.

Before she could match Blanca, another face swam into focus, that of the Adjacker Dollar Llama. Llama was an elusive man who had created software that could jack into random users via a virus that overrode Bits and Bytes protocol in order to inject an ad for his products. In this way, he could sell with very little credit dispersal. He sold a line of plasmold spinning lighted balls on sticks called Glitterati. Atop the spinning balls sat a large, bald, plastic, shirtless, seated man who was grinning. They sold well, due to the fact that they lit up and spun.

They also sold well because adjacks were very effective. In fact, once infected, the user had only to buy the Glitterati to get the randomly inserted ads to stop. Kenda had been thus far able to resist buying one, so the ads kept showing up, every once in a while. She just tried to learn to live with it. The only downside is that these jacked ads did not respond to erasure or dissolution by shaking her head or refocusing-you had to watch them or buy the product.

The ad began inside her mind. She sat still and watched it.

"...Sparkle and shine,
Dollar Llama Glitterati,
it spins allotti
Sparkle and shine,
You'll have a good time!
Sparkle and shine,
You'll have a good time,
It spins and shines!
It spins alotti-Glitterati
Sparkle and shine...

It played 14 times, each time the tempo increased, getting faster and faster and then it abruptly disappeared. Kenda waited until she stopped humming the tune and shook her head and refocused the test on the internal mental display.

She looked at the Newsporters on her mindscreen, trying to peer past their vacant gazes to find anything to link them to their bios and parshals. Something that might distinguish them beyond their hair, but she could not. Their faces were a wave of scars. Eyes and noses every distinguishing characteristic fell away as her attention wavered, so did the focus of the image until they became a blurry sea that melded and molded, responding to Kenda's mind movements, as she struggled to keep them separated and reassemble the individual pictures. Soon, there was just a screen filled with featureless faces and distorted smiles, full of hair and teeth.

Her screen flashed, "Do you wish to retake the exam?"

🕮 Intersections of Chance

Several years ago, long before Kenda failed her test, deep within the P_ear console production facility, a computer operator named Puhc monitored the production of the consoles. He hoped one day to get into an infopairing degree program so he wouldn't have to work so hard. He could just send newsports and parshals and EEMs all day and his rent and food would be paid for. He had not been approved for the P_ear program because he couldn't make connections-he had failed all the Information Pairing pre-exams, which deemed him, *"incapable of forming connections between situations, products and emotion."*

"Someday," he thought, "I will be a pairer. I will be a newsporter." He stroked his stringy yellow hair color with red stripes. When you had to pay for your own hair color, choices were limited, but nobody except the Spine went natch-uncolored-natural. Phuc, like most people feared going natch because of its association with the Spine from the old nursree rhyme,

"Beware the Brown Hair! Murderers and thieves,

knives at their knees! Natch! Beware the Brown Hair!

Black cloaked, eyes red, Spine bring death..."

Right now, like most times, he wasn't thinking anything at all. He was playing Throws. He looked up as a roar resounded through the otherwise quiet workspace. Throws had been interrupted by a message on his standard worker-issue wrist P_ear screen; it flashed an error message and continued to blink red. The production line had stopped and he smelled the vile braking chemical that was expelled when the mechanism had to stop suddenly. It belched out in one grey-black puff. The message on his wrist screen reported that it had finished its analysis and that there was an error in a connector on one of the units.

He went over, picked the offending unit off the line. He looked at the unit, and it looked ok, but the error message reported that it had a slow leak in the emotional transfer grid. His eyes couldn't detect the hairline crack in there, but he squinted at it anyway. He was required to fail it, so that it could be repaired. He did not remember the proper protocol when a unit failed and couldn't get in trouble again or he'd be fired. He knew he had to do something about sending a repair file. He racked his brains to try to remember what to do. He opened a manual on her wrist unit. He was trying to find the unit failure code. As he stood there wondering what to do, his eyes popped open.

He smiled and set the unit back on the conveyance. He did not know the unit failure code and he did not like looking things up, but he *did* know the override code. He punched it in on his wrist unit. The conveyance revved up again and the unit, and its faulty Emotional Transfer Grid rushed off for delivery and installation, for User: Harkonna311371 to be exact.

Puhc sat back down. He tapped at his wrist screen and pulled up his EEMs to try to earn some credits...

OUTGOING...Thin Banana, it's thin, it's for thin people, you will thin, you will happy.... 00.00003 credits awarded...

...People use Eliass Family door buttons for that down home ding dong...00.0003 credits awarded.

Puhc smiled at a funny word. He kept tapping off credits.

Soon, the taps and the ticks of P_ear units flying by created a rhythm- making a disturbing mechanical heartbeat, echoing in the otherwise empty room.

❧ Intersection of Insurance/Interest

"Where was the rage? A soft net, a gilded cage, and slow boil. These things soften our perceptions, benign evil treads lightly, but carries the same threat." –Jernull, Public Archives

Kenda pulled up her celebrity test and reasserted the celebrity faces by shaking her head. She was about to retest when she was interrupted by the sound of beeping. It was the familiar alert showing missed EEM notifications that manifested themselves inside her head. She shut them down without reviewing them and was docked 32.5 credits for doing so. She slapped the credit warning off as well. But there was another noise in her apartment that her sleep-addled brain couldn't place. She got up off the floor.

The front doorpanel. Someone was knocking on it, which could only mean it was Jernull; he was the only one who knocked. Everyone else used the EEM system to send a *Knockalert-Let someone know you're there.* They only did this because more often than not the *Eliass Family Buttons-Old fashioned buttons for that down home ding dong* did not work. Still, no one ever knocked, no one but Jernull.

She heard his voice through the thin door-"Can I come in, Kenda? I discovered something and I need to tell someone."

"Yes, of course, I've been trying to EEM you."

Jernull came in, waded through a pile of Thinbanana casings and sat down nervously on the SympaticoCouch- he looked as if he hadn't eaten or slept in days, which isn't abnormal for him, but there was a (haunted) look about him that gave Kenda pause, or it would have if she had known the word. She used, in her mind, the only word she could think of-thin. Thin. She had no other word. Something forced itself to the forefront of her consciousness and she expressed it without hesitation, on automatic.

"Can I get you a ThinBanana?" 12.3 credits appeared on her mindscreen at the natural mention of the brand, along with a warning because she did not repeat the tagline-*"the thin banana for thin people."* She tapped the console to remove the banner readout from her psyche. It flashed red and was immediately replaced by the cheery thank you message reporting that the 12.3 credits were used to pay the balance of her foodstuffs credit this month.

She shook her head to remove the message, "Jernull, what is going on?" She sat down beside him.

"Your emotional readout is—frustration! Wow, have a sleep and rid yourself of—transmission cancelled by user."

"Listen," he said, "I feel like I am on to something and I don't know anyone else to talk to. I've been working on classifying tangential theories and studying them for further grouping-remember?"

Kenda nodded.

"Anyway, I discovered these connections, and I don't know what they mean, just that they-these threads- exist, but not what their intersections mean."

"OK..."- Kenda nodded comprehension and motioned for him to continue. She wondered what it would be like if he were to touch her face. Unconsciously, her hand went out toward him in an awkward gesture that neither of them understood. She lowered it and moved closer to him on the Sympaticouch, waiting for him to continue.

"OK, well the theory rallies around the same main idea-that of interest. Interest can be broken down further into insurance. Essentially, everything, and I mean everything can be built from raw parts and translated into how it ensures something else against another component in the system. Try me, if you don't believe it."

"Tell you something?"

"Yes! Just say anything and I'll prove that it doesn't exist outside the threads of Insurance and Interest."

"Ok. What about friends." Kenda looked hopeful.

"Insurance against not having someone to cluster cast with and do product resends with."

"Interesting pairing. I was trying pair love with something other than products. Like people."

Jernull sat back. The SympaticoCouch powered up and a hot flash shot up both of their backs. *"Emotion recognized! You both are experiencing ecs —"*

Kenda's face grew hot and she quickly shook off the announcement. Jernull looked at his hands and rubbed them on his pantlegs. She coughed.

Then he looked up and met her green eyes with his blue-grey ones. "I-I have thought of that. I-I feel like, I like certain people more than other people. I just have no way of understanding why that happens." They both felt another warm surge from the couch and an increasing pressure from every piece of the SympaticoCouch frame that moved them closer together.

"Emotion analyzed---"

Kenda tapped to disable it, she had never been so hot in her life. The couch squeezed harder, not registering the signal. She wondered what Jernull's emotional transfer setting was. This was the most extreme feedback she'd ever gotten from the SympaticoCouch.

She hummed and tried to spur the conversation away from the couch, "Hmm, hmm-so, where does interest come in? What were you saying?"

Jernull stood and paced, wading through the colored debris clusters strewn everywhere, but kept oddly closer to Kenda than he had planned, almost hovering. "I think it is intersection of love and people, like the Workers, uhh, non-pairers, do."

"The Workerlove, that is an intersection?"

This time it was Jernull's face that flushed. "I think it is. They know each other well, live with each other and...they are together, so they influence each other. Intersection of lives."

"Intersection of lives. But what about people wholly disconnected from one another? Strangers."

"That's even easier!" His hands quivered, and he sat next to her, very close to her. As he continued, gentle vibrations from the SympaticoCouch shook them both, and they avoided meeting each other's eyes. "We all walk around thinking people who don't know us have no interest in us. We think that is true because why else would someone want good or ill or nil from any of us if they scarcely knew of our existence? Well, something always intersects! They want. We want. Somewhere their living or their healthstuff or their something has been put in our path and they see us as an obstacle to their object of interest, we become not another being, but a wall, like 'I don't care about you, so I don't care if I hurt you.'"

"If you know someone, you may have an easier time seeing them as a known and thereby creating a new thread of interest called, "I don't want to hurt that person I know." and that complicates the intersection of the two competing interests by adding another thread. But when you don't know them, that thread doesn't exist, so you could hurt that person, there is less complicating that structure. We need systems that interrupt those threads. Look at the newsports. They have an interest that intersects with our interest to know. And this is where it gets weird."

Jernull leaned in to Kenda and covered both of their transmission sensors, muting them. He whispered to her, "I saw a Spine being beaten by the Footmen."

"Real Spine? Where? When? How did you know it was—well you know-them both?" Kenda was more than mildly aware of his warm hand near her cheek. The couch clicked on and Kenda waved it off.

"Brown hair, long cloak, just like the nursree rhymes. But the Footm- but the men were hitting her." Jernull felt the warmth of her cheek; he could barely keep his thoughts right, something he never had difficulty with before. "Uhh, but, uhh later, I never saw any report about a Spine being beaten and yet it happened. If there is other news, we do not know because no one tells us about it. I mean, if the Spine are such a menace, then why don't we ever hear about them except in old nursree rhymes and ads to sell new colors of Cutichrome?"

"But you saw it."

"Yes, and not a single newsport featured it, it has been two weeks now and nothing. Something that major would or should be on the newsports." Jernull felt dizzy.

He was still covering the external inputs on both of their consoles, trying to keep his focus on what he was saying. This shining light-listening and understanding-flowed between them.

Kenda forced herself to look at him, past his azure blue bangs; he did not meet her gaze. His ideas moved her-the words. She managed, "What does it mean?"

"Interest, is all I can figure. Someone is interested in not having that revealed, Spine or Footmen- I cannot find the words to describe it. But one of them has need of some insurance against not having it revealed. That insurance affects others, like you and I who have an interest to know, but cannot get the information we want. I think that if someone can separate interest and insurance from things that happen-in the telling of things-there will be a closer, umm, closer version of things, like in a report, if I tell you these things apart from interest and insurance, they are more closer to the thing as they are. It would be pairing turning on a light to see things better, showing a thing, making a newsport of a thing to know it better."

"Wow, I have never heard that pairing before. Light to seeing things to knowing things truly. What about my pairing? People to love, but like, without advertiser partnership marriage."

"I think advertiser partner marriages are…" .He released their feeds and his hand immediately felt the cold of the air, missing where it had just been. He paused and looked at his fingers, "They are…uhh, you see--I am scheduled to partner marry Kitty Reed next week for 3 weeks. After that, I am supposed to partner marry Blanca Rudio or one of her cats, I am not sure which one, Ceramicat or real cat. These marriages do increase credits and sales, but I don't really like them. But non-pairers, workers, get to marry anyone. They don't have the level of interests in brandsponsors. I don't know. I'd rather…be without so many interests. I would rather…"

"Yes?"

"Pairing is two…next to…I don't know how to…" He faltered for the right words.

In a gesture of considerable faith, Jernull, knelt on one knee before Kenda and placed himself as close to her as he dared. Such advances were thought to be common, a worker trait, not done amongst the elite pairers. He could not meet her eyes, but felt a soft hand under his chin and he let Kenda raise his eyes level with hers and she leaned in to him.

Without a breath, they kissed.

Kenda felt the Sympaticouch struggle to ascertain the torrent that raged from her faulty unit, and his amplified one. As a result, every circuit in the couch overloaded and fizzed out.

There was a moment that held with silence, and a great deal of inexplicable heat. Somehow, they had both stood, moved closer, such that no plane of existence was visible between them. Both their eyes were closed.

Neither of them could have been counted on to know if the world continued to exist in this spacious moment that dragged and dreamed on its own. It formed a reality so durable that it could never leave their minds entirely, ever again.

From the end of that moment, from the death-like closeness of both their minds, an advertisement blared a warning—*please have your P_ear console checked for Emotional Transfer Grid leaks, sensors indicate overloads on all connections! Footmen have been notified and will record this anomaly…*

They both reached up at the same time and slapped the notice away, silencing it. Jernull tapped the motions for double delete for both of them, so it wouldn't get filed with the Footmen.

Jernull stepped away awkwardly, making odd, incoherent excuses for leaving, "I have to go-I have to meet with my paternal figure at his office about the speech he wants me to give at the Miss Info Pageant, and I am already really late." He hunched over her side table as if he were depositing or adjusting something, then fumbled with the door release and was gone. Something intangible lingered in the room; whatever it was, began to severely affect the fried SympaticoCouch circuitry.

When the door slid shut, Kenda fell backward deep in the SympatiCouch where she lay still for a long time with her eyes half lidded.

Her mind filled with the thoughts that he had given her.

"Insurance against not knowing." She thought. "Interests get in the way of knowing."

There was something else that Jernull had said to her-a while ago. She let her saved memories flood into her mind and sifted through them to play the one that had their first meeting. She focused on it and it played into view. It was a year ago at the COOLWALK! café on campus, and he was coming to meet her to be her tutor. The first time they met, he approached her table and said, without greeting her, "I have 10 minutes and 20 sends to make my monthly quota, which is more important to my newscasts? Many or much content?"

"Many sends and much content are important, but what will get you to the send quota is many sends."

Jernull replied, "Yes. Who made this model famous with Ceramicat?"

"Blanca Rudio."

Jernull nodded, "Give me a pairing for ThinBanana that you would use for friends at a coffee shop."

"Oh. How about "Many thin people use Thin Banana to stay thin, but it also is good for eating with Shugso, then you'll be thinpopular!"

Jernull smiled and sat down across from Kenda.

"That's a good pairing. I have never heard that one before."

"Really? I could try again, I could review the forms and try again."

"No, I think it's a good pairing. Straying from form will help you become a better newsporter. They want new things."

"I thought you were supposed to change the forms around, but stay within them."

"That's what everyone tells you in pre-pairing. But, I think true pairing is a process to make the forms into another thing, but most people can't do it, in fact, I am one of the only candidates in recent memory that has done it, well, besides you." Jernull smiled.

She had looked at Jernull unsure of how to respond to such a thing. As an Information Paring Major she had heard all the stories of Jernull, his famously credit-rich paternal figure, his work in the pairing field -she knew he'd be different, Dayzee had already told her that, because she had been tutored by him before and even had brandsponsor partner married him once.
"But, what could be said in response to a statement like that?"

"True pairing?"

"A pairing so remarkable that it becomes its own thing."

"I am sorry, Mister Banburn-"

"Jernull."

"Jernull...but I don't see why what I did was good."

"You made something."

"Yes, I made a pairing that did not follow prescribed forms."

"No, you made some *thing*. Listen- anytime a pairing of two things makes a certain level of matching, it becomes another thing entirely, something, new. A third thing from a two. Can you understand that?"

"I guess not."

"Did they ever show you maths?"

"Yes, once."

"What is 1 and 1?"

"Twove?"

"No, that is 11 and 1."

"I was nervous, I meant two?"

"Yes, two."

"Now what is two and one more?"

"Two and another, two and another, umm Threve?"

"Three, yes."

"I feel silly, I haven't done maths in a long time."

"Don't you count your apart-ment credits?"

"No, gaw, no. The counterpiece app does that."

"What if it is wrong?"

"The counterpiece is programmed from the factories, they can't be wrong. But—," Kenda concentrated, "my Winraise isn't working either and the company said it can't break yet, but, still, it *is* broken."

"What if someone had a desire in them being wrong or in not replacing something that is broken?"

"I guess I wouldn't know it."

"I haven't figured that out yet, but I am working on it. So, back to the matter of maths-take one and one and one and you've got 3, right?" Kenda nodded and Jernull continued, "Yes, so, 1 thing compared to 1 thing makes a descriptor of a third thing, a new thing. You just made a new thing. I have people studying with me that cannot go beyond the forms that they are given, coupling and recoupling forms that have been used for years."

"The pairing is new if it has not been paired before, right?"

"I don't think it is possible to use the forms and do that, but you just paired a word with another and got that new result. What is your name again?"

"Kenda of Brandsponsor Snakeoil Skinshine. Lotions! *Try Snakeoils, it's ssssuper!*" Kenda mechanically tossed her hair to make the snake overlay slither behind her ear in showy display of the full-featured animated nanophotons- a display of the wealth that her position with her brandsponsor gave her.

Jernull winced. "Please, it is not necessary at sessions with me to earn credits. I wish you wouldn't do your taglines."

"All right, but listen, you were once partner married to a friend of mine, Dayzee, she told me you loved taglines."

"I-I used to write them, but no, I don't like them. They make me tired, I guess. Dayzee? I don't remember her. I have been paired so many times."

Kenda lowered her shoulders. She had been nervous about meeting Jernull, given his status in a huge corporation, but he was nothing like she'd been told.

She felt the heat, from the SolarFlair green light waves that were projecting over the Coffee House! for the Festival of the Credit celebration later today.

She leaned toward him; she wanted to hear everything he had to say.

"Tell me more. I want to know."

Jernull launched into his theory about the way a thing could be brought into the world using other words, like new words, new pairings. Kenda listened and replied, assimilating his theories into her mind. It was difficult, but she managed well. What prevented her from giving her full attention was that she kept attempting to make eye contact with his clear, grey-blue eyes behind the 5-inch azure Cutichrome bangs. They were tinted the colors of his father's company, Bits and Bytes Blue, with orange P_ear logo overlays that blinked on and off. Occasionally, as he spoke, he absently tapped his bangs so they self-tucked out of the way and his eyes lit on hers in various awkward moments throughout the conversation. It brought up an emotion in her. What it was-she couldn't quite say. There was something to be said between them, that they had no words for. She only knew she wanted more of the words-the conversation.

The memory faded. She shook her head again to refocus. She looked around the room to reorient herself to the external world and her eyes fell on her side table. Jernull had left something.

She walked over to look. It had words on it-written in Chocospread! He had used the spread to put an EEM into physical form on the smooth surface of a Thinbanana. She looked down at the words. She had never seen words outside of those that appeared in her mindscreen.

These were words in the physical world. She marveled at this, and traced her fingers through the hardened spread.

"How like him," she thought. She read the wording out loud, "Will you come with me to the Miss Info pageant?" She smiled and re-traced the letters in dried Chocospread.

In truth, she didn't like the Missy awards. Even with the rumors that she might be the candidate in the next award cycle, she didn't know if she could be a part of it. "Maybe I have other interests that are separate, but, what?" She said aloud to no one and it shocked her a bit.

No one talked like him. No one acted like him, but she couldn't stop herself from seeking him out. He didn't get his ideas from school; she knew that. They had almost kicked him out after his Billy story directing fiasco. It was only due to his powerful paternal figure, the founder of Banburn University, that he was able to remain in school.

She stood there in the dark, crunching on the wafer-thin, dry, pasty-crushed-pressed-meal-partial-snack-stuff and felt a deep desire to help Jernull more with his theory. He was right about one thing- there was a something in the intersections and interest he talked about.

Her P_ear blared without warning, an advertisement broadcast along with a short vidCast-CANDY LANE AND THE IMMACULATE ORCASM- A COLLECTION OF OLDIES FROM HER GOLD AND BOLD ALBUM, FEATURING HER HIT SINGLES:

LOVING YOUR DIGITAL READOUT

SOUL OF MY SCREEN-BUTTONS OF MY HEART

AND HER MULTI-PLATINUM REMIX…

THUMBING YOUR NOSE AT THE SUN—

The advertisement voice boomed—**buy the greatest compilation of songs made in the last millennia**, here's a sample from *Thumbing your Nose at the Sun* archived by the good people at the Digital Universal Management Project…

Some people think it's rude
To grow a son in a vacuum tube.
And some people think its dum
To thumb your nose at the sun.
Those people think a lot
Some people do, not, not, not.
They wait, they listen
To hear a pot to pissen.
Drop the bread
a path to the dead
found by one
who thumbs his nose at the sun!
Some see society
of dark disgrace,
but I see lighted grays.
I see lighted grays.
I see lighted grays.
I see lighted grace.

Kenda tapped her console and the voice went dead.

"Oh farce, Dayzee." Dayzee was the only one she knew that would send her a Candy Lane advertisement, she was a freak for Gold and Bold and her only friend who considered herself the ancient digitized music scene queen. Without knowing it, she hummed the last line of the song; she replayed it unconsciously in her memory frame. She did not have a clue what it meant by lighted grace. As the light of day pulsed in through her window again, she dressed, and headed out to Themall to find Dayzee.

🐾 The Twitch

"This is for the archives. What do you remember before you came to us. Tell me about The Twitch."

"You know about it?" Kenda asked.

The Spine acolyte named RiEF adjusted the recording equipment that transcribed the interview onto DNA strands printing out into a tube below the table. "Yes, but only our own horror. I need to know how it registers from someone who has actually been around them, up close. Tell me whatever you remember." She finished setting up the machine and sat down next to Kenda and nodded.

"Push People are post-Twitch; that comes after, I mean. That is, I am guessing. I am trying to blend my memories with the information I have access to now, but back then, when I was a user, we—uhh—didn't think about trying to assimilate information like that. We just used the Push for our own amusement...to us, they were little more than moveable, poseable things. I came to know the full horror about them only at the end when my grid was failing. And now, of course."

"Describe what you felt when you first saw Dayzee Twitch."

"I can't tell you how long she had it because it is so gradual, but I knew for sure that day that I went to see her at Themall. Enough Twitch in a system causes disintegration into Push. From Push, it can either be a slow or quick descent into Blank, but in the end, the morg, uhh death is... that is, the transition to morg is very disturbing."

"Yes, I have seen this transition. There is often blood."

"This is hard. I feel...shame, is that the right word?"

"Yes, that works. You can take your time." RiEF waited patiently for Kenda to try to continue. She moved her hands from the recording activator, to show Kenda that she was in no hurry, "It is important that others know this, but only if or when you can."

"Twitching is not good, even though most senders thought it was fun. I don't think that most people really paired well that the morg comes from having Twitch, like denial. I remember the day at Themall with Dayzee."

Kenda urged the memory on, but it was at great cost to herself that she relayed it. Kenda's normally taut mouth on her face, flatlined and her eyes closed, lost in a real and powerful memory.

It was the day after she and Jernull had kissed that she had walked, wading through the ever-present litter of product casings, over to meet Dayzee at Themall. She was suppressing the tug of her mind, as it bleated out EEMs *(SolarFlair! Make it Funlight!)* and credit announcements *(you need 56 taglines by your next recharge to keep your overlay upgrades this cycle! Thank you for promoting Thinbanana! Thinmeals for thin people, try our new purple flavor!)*. She felt like she hadn't gotten a thing done yesterday, she'd even skipped her final re-take. She couldn't focus on things. Except for Jernull. Kess? No, that's not right-he had kissed her the day before. That is the word for it. She *had* felt something- an otherness she didn't know how to categorize, that lingered. She shook her head and tried to dislodge this sensation that was working on her.

Up ahead of her, under a sage green Funlight, Dayzee smiled behind an enormous pink, orange, yellow and black bin with the new product, Honeyplugs Popnchews dripping out of it. Dayzee tossed her one and Kenda chewed it. She tried to spit it out in disgust, but it dribbled off her lips and slopped right back into her mouth.

"Ucks! Why does it do that?"

"It is Honeyplugs new Popnchews, they won't let you spit it out because they dispense instant permanent credits. Once you "popnchew" you have to swallow the whole thing down. Don't worry though, its honey- coated to go down easier. Swallow, you'll see."

Kenda swallowed quickly. "Hmm, that does make it easier. Tasty, except for the beginning part. What makes it go back in your mouth?"

"Tendrils? Of umm...material, nanoparticulate, or something ...bacterium? I forget. But it has the cutest aftereffect. Go ahead, burp."

Kenda tried to burp and a pink puff of smoke came out with a smiling CeramiCat's face outlined in the cloud.

Dayzee clapped. "See! It is a double credit campaign, that's why the instant permanent credit. First, the bad taste, then it goes down smooth with honey-coating, then a fun ad in smoke!!!"

Kenda felt her stomach lurch. She vomited only to have the very unpleasant aftereffect of most of the vomit slamming back into her mouth and onto her face and clothes. She leaned against the Honeyplugs booth to catch herself.

Dayzee patted her back, "I would keep it down because the next time is usually diarrhea. Here, eat a ThinBanana-*the thin banana for thin people!*- I heard the potsium in them helps calm throwups." Dayzee tapped off credits for her Thinbanana repeats.

Kenda gobbled the Thinbanana and clicked off the Honeyplugs Popnchews credit, the Ceramicat cloud credit and the Thin Banana credits, even without the taglines, she was 35 credits ahead again. A credit report sounded in her head, *You are well under way to make your credits for the day! You didn't repeat your taglines, though! Keep repeating, keep credits, keep eating! Keep repeating, keep credits, keep eating! Keep repeating, keep credits, keep eating!*

Kenda slapped off the credit alert and cleaned her clothes off with some wetnaps that apparently come standard in every Popnchew wrapper. She shook her mindscreen away and noticed Dayzee tilting. Dayzee grabbed Kenda's arm and her head arched sideways.

Kenda looked at Dayzee in what might have been horror had she known that word then. Abject terror, would have fit better. Kenda could tell that Dayzee was about to Twitch. "Oh, I feel it. EEMs are coming. I can feel it."

She began to quiver, shaking all over and her eyes bore into Kenda with a ferocity, as she whispered, "They are coming...the EEMs...do you feel it?"

Vibrations shot through her body and she reached for her console in a wide pantomime. Her eyes glazed over. She blinked once, heavy, slow lidded and wearily... "They are here..."

Kenda realized that she was holding her breath and staring. At once Dayzee refocused, and said, "What did you need to ask me?"

She did not want to tell Dayzee about how she felt about the Honeyplugs Popnchews-she could not afford credit loss for negative product responses so she avoided it altogether. Instead, she brought up why she had come here. "Dayzee, Jernull and I...I...think I might marry him."

"Great, it is good for product cross-branding; it worked out great for me, I picked up two sponsors and we were only married two weeks, or something like that. I figured you'd marry him next year when you might be crowned MissInfo. By the way Popnchews are great for when you need to show off a product, they are a pairer's, umm...useful to...umm...good for...you can get the smoke to say anything." Dayzee slapped off her brand mention credits.

"No, I mean, I want to marry him, like workers do. For Ever."

"Popnchews can make a special promotion better, whatever product, whatever brand!" Dayzee slapped off more credits, "Then how will you rebrand yourself to pay for new venues, foodstuffs and apart-ments?"

"I...don't know...work?."

"Bad news! Another good thing Popnchews were made for! *Bad news goes down with the sweet puff of instant permanent credits to follow!*" Dayzee slapped off the credits and her quota banked 69 credits with a shower of stars in her mind. She smiled smugly.

Kenda felt sick again and nibbled the Thinbanana. "He kissed me."

"Anyway, you know what can take the taste of that kiss out of your mouth? Honeyplugs P--"

Kenda turned and walked away. She left Dayzee mid-sentence. Her stomach hurt, her throat was raw, and she was still brushing smeared Honeyplugs out of her hair. It took her several minutes to get the last of it out. She decided she would EEM Dayzee a "Gotta run" apology later if she felt like paying the ApologyEEM credit, which cost as much as she made standing there getting her own vomit thrown back in her face.

🐾 Dayzee's Day, See?

Anyone walking down the Coolwalk! was subject to its "Areas of Activation", so called because massive amounts of credit opps could be aggressively sent to users that owed credits. Such was Dayzee's problem that day, just before she was supposed to meet Kenda at Themall. The Twitch was settling in her psyche, but hadn't yet infiltrated her system, so most of the EEMs got through without causing her to Twitch...but they most certainly didn't help.

The ads began as soon as she set one foot down on the Coolwalk! ...

"Tell everyone about new BARscar control, Advanced coating and image repair, for a fraction of the credits those other oils charge!!! BARscar beats the bruising every time!"

"Don't know what to say? Say it with Easy TAG. We boost your tagline repeats even while you sleep. There is nowhere we can't tag from! Don't waste your time thinking-activate us today!"

"PraySay. A new product that says your prayers for you. Thanks every Gaw for everything and comes with free candies. Stop by any PraySay vendor to get your candies now. And don't worry, PraySay comes in two types of sincerity modes, so it will sound just like you are doing it! PraySay, say your prayers and mean it with PraySay!"

"TapALONG, LED flashing lights permanently embedded in your fingernails! Now people can see and hear you tap! TapALONG!"

Dayzee tapped in an appointment to get some TapAlongs installed as the ad continued,

"Also available with alternating color lights,

colors and tapping-all in one,

major surgery required, but think of the fun!

They're the shiniest, they are great!

And they come with a 20 credit rebate.

Think of all the credits you'll save with this!

Get 'em, buy 'em, they're the best!"

Dayzee nodded at the ad she had heard 250 times that week and thought, "Think of all the credits I'll save!"

Dayzee's head twitched, but only slightly. Another EEM was coming, and it was just out of range. The blare of ads abruptly stopped when she stepped off the Coolwalk! and entered Themall. She walked, ankle deep in litterwaste from labels and product casings, over to pick up her Honeyplugs Popnchews sample bin.

Dayzee's condition was just like the typical onset of the Twitch. The infected user's console would anticipate the exact moment that an incoming EEM would arrive, sometimes cocking their head to one side, eyes rolling up, sometimes patting their hands on their pants pockets or looking around as if listening, or even sometimes flexing their thumbs or shivering slightly. It would be followed by a feeling of extreme pride, the user was unaware that the boost in their esteem had increased, but a warm, vacant euphoria would wash over them. It would consume their consciousness entirely. Once the EEM passed they would snap back to their surroundings, only vaguely aware of the entire incident.

In its end stages, the Twitch was much worse. During the last phases, the user simply turned inward so many times, they never came back-they simply blacked out, went Push.

When people first observed their friends coming down with it, they made it a game; they would do massive group sends to a person developing the Twitch and vidcast the results of the person freezing and writhing, twitching. If that user stopped responding, no one asked questions. If they suddenly stopped showing up at Meetingplace, no one looked for them because there were lots of things to vidcast, and lots of things to watch and to send and resend.

Dayzee moved her Honeyplugs bin into place. She smoothed her clothes. She dutifully waved at passersby. She sent and resent everything she heard about her product. Her voice was sweet and even. Her hair was self-tucked into place. However, several times during that morning, awaiting Kenda's arrival, her one eye would close and she would ever so slightly twitch.

Just before Kenda stopped at her bin, Dayzee's torso wavered as if blessing the scene in a rhythmic homage, her mouth opened slightly and pulled back in a grimace to the right side and her head twitched slightly to the left. She tapped her pants pockets and narrowed her eyes, drooling out the words, "…An EEM is coming… I know it… there it is…if I focus I can read it before it gets here…"

Her eyes glazed over and her gaze settled again as her face and neck and head melted back into their former relaxed state, "Whooo…umm yes, so hey, Kenda, what's good?"

Kenda stared at Dayzee who seemed not to have noticed that she just Twitched. Kenda did not want to tell her, twitching was a novelty to all who have never seen its end game. But Kenda had seen someone Morg.

🕊 The Push People

Kenda put her head in her hands and wept.

RiEF let her recover before continuing. She gave her a drink and some food. When she looked to be regaining herself, she asked her, "What other details do you remember about the transition from Twitch to Push?"

"I don't remember who first started using the words Push People. We thought it was funny to send VidCasts of them. They will move wherever you put them. They will hold whatever you put in their hands. Some people cut their hair or dressed them or undressed them. They don't respond and their consoles blink so slowly. There is a grinding sound, a thin, hollow sound of something spinning around inside their consoles. If you alert the Baggers, you earn credits. They don't talk. They only move when you steer them and provide the motion with your own strength. They stay where you leave them, unless...unless they are left in the throughways and the trams run them over...or..."

"They are taken?"

"Yes. If someone reports them to the baggers or the Footmen find them and call in the Baggers. Bag and zip and ship." Oh, gaw, Radka." Kenda swept aside tears, sniffed and faced RiEF.

"Is there a better—another word for the Push?"

"We had another word, Comatoes. I have searched the archives; there isn't a word for this, or I haven't spelled it right. It is new, I think."

"Yes, a kind of new. There were similar things like this, but never exactly this. The search term you need is coma. Continue."

"Once a user is blank or morg, can they come back?"

"Theorhetically, yes, but we haven't ever been able to."

"You've tried?"

"Many times. Your knowledge of the emotional side of it is what we are trying to record, though. Our study has been limited to the clinical side. I know the loss that you speak of is not new at all."

"Grief. Mourning. To suffer. Do you think the Push suffer?"

"I don't know if they can register pain, but there is another consideration that harms the people that abuse them.

"I see that clearly now. Using. That bad. Shame. Indignity...and one other word...inhumane. The archives you gave me had a word, disgrace?"

"That's a good one; read up on that one. What you speak of, I see it in your face now. Just tell me of anything you remember."

"I think they *can* feel pain. Oh-" Kenda winced. The strain was unbearable. She knew it was the right thing to do-share this story-but it didn't lessen the pain any. In the midst of this, she wondered how to lessen the pain for these people and an idea struck her. Maybe when she could find Jernull, he could try to reset Dayzee's substrate matrix to a Pre-Twitch infection state. She would mention this to RiEF later. Right now, she focused to get this story right...

"There was a Push that morged in front of us at the coffeehouse MeetingPlace. I don't know his name, but he was being used to make a game. He was short. He had speckled hair that blinked on and off. He was overdue to upgrade the nanoparticulates in his hair, and also, much of his hair had begun falling out. His body was at a permanent tilt, from being bent over so much. We put product in his hands and pushed him to each other. Many more people joined the game and his legs stumbled. Back and forth he would totter and wobble. We traded credits for how far he would go for each push. We vidcast the game and other people bet on it too. With each push from a user, he seemed less able to stay up. His expression never changed. It was stuck permanently in some silly grin. He dropped product all over the place, creams, and spreads, anything that anyone shoved in his hands.

Bang after bang, each time he would hit a wall or scrape his knees bloody against a product display box, we would smile, not even laughing, just grinning and sending out vidCasts, until some people began pushing him together-many hands-too much force. That poor Push, I mean being-human. He slid on some spilled cream and into the path of an oncoming tram. We all watched. We all vidCast it. He fell over, but not like he did previously. He was going so fast. His face split. His console fell out, and the blood began to seep and mix with the product wrappers on the ground. We were still vidCasting. Then the comments came in, "Ucks."

"That was Cooltastic!"

"Great PUSH!"

"Morg to Pushies"

"That looks like Mildin. He Twitched out a few days ago."

"It probably *is* Mildin-you kicat."

"I called the Baggers. I get the credit for the Bag and Ship."

"I tapped the Baggers. *I* get the credit for the Bag and Ship."

Mildin, or whoever it was, just lay there. Half his face smashed up into his hair. Then the tram came. Over the speakers in our consoles the announcement came for rainfall. Overhead, the light changed to a dull Funlight that indicated rainfall. Everyone scattered to find a place indoors. No one stayed to watch the Baggers, but me. I waited behind the product display boxes. It took them hours to get him bagged. There were so many pieces.

Just as they were finishing up, I heard Footmen approach, their boots clanking. The console near Mildin's head had popped out, but it was still attached with strands of slick veins and microtubing. They picked it up, it went blue and tripped out to black. I ran. I just wanted to be near anyone that still had their face. His light was blue, so-he must have still been feeling something.

Kenda stopped talking. She put a hand on the table in front of her. RiEF stopped the archive recorder and extended a square of cloth toward Kenda, who took it and bowed her head.

Tears were streaking her face and dropping steadily on her lap. Her body began to show the full weight of this knowledge. A little knowledge keeps a person guessing, but knowing the fullness of a thing-to come to knowledge this way-the full harm-the complete narrative weighs heavily.

Kenda found herself, "WHY?" Her breath became quick and sobs heaved within her, "He could feel. He could feel! Before the morg, he was sensing. The Push are still living and sensing, but—oh farce! What is the word…" Kenda turned her head aside and looked up. She twisted the cloth. The right words from the saved archive assimilated to her conscious mind.

"Torment. Torture."

"We used our devices and our actions against a feeling being. We treated him like a thing."

RiEF nodded. "This kind of revelation requires perspective."

"What can we do?"

She looked for comfort from RiEF, who responded by nodding. It was clear that the set of her jaw softened. She was the embodiment of duty and sorrow. The lines on her face reflecting the pain Kenda related. She knew.

"We can plan. We can form a response. We work towards freedom through knowledge as is our mandate, but this work is slow in the face of sheer quantity. As a new member of Spine, you can make this your mandate, too. That is why we need this information, to know is to be warned. This is what we do."

"Recording and planning is good. Maintaining the archives is good, but there is the final component that seems begged here-acting."

RiEF fairly winced. The word seemed to take a piece of her. "I'm sorry, RiEF. I don't mean to say that you do nothing."

"We are split on this. Our unilateral actions centuries ago, nearly had disastrous results. We have to be careful, but-" RiEF leaned in, "There is no one who wants war, the archives are full of those lessons, but there is certainly a wider range of options than archiving and war."

"Whenever we get there, I am in." Kenda accessed the word grateful in her archives and tried to recall the other day that she thought would be helpful. "I can tell you about what happened to Radka. When I saw her transition from Push to Morg.

RiEF began the recording again onto the DNA strands for posterity. The files were named. Radka, UserPyter2204, Transition Push to Morg, Spine Archives, as related by Acolyte XY-Kenda Iteration.

"The day that I saw Radka morg. I remember there was lots of grey-black Funlight, not many sponsors will purchase Funlight when rainfall is scheduled and that day rainfall was scheduled..."

Kenda poured the story forth, the memories sparking within her.

She said she had spent a few hours on a charging wall, and divided the rest of her time pairing and sending. She left the Juicewall—*We fill you up when you are running down!* She moved past the crowds at the CoffeeHouse often having to paw her way through the crowd to smear the rest of her Skinshine Snakeoils product on others, repeating the mandatory tagline as she went, "Try Skinshine, It's SSSSSSSSSUPER". Credits mounted on the screen of her mind with each tag repeat. She was weary, as she headed back to her apart-ment when she came across some workers standing around in a semi-circle.

As she drew closer, she realized it was Baggers hovering around something. It happened to be a body on the ground. It looked like a posed Push, stuck in the last position someone had left them in. Upon getting a closer look, Kenda realized that it was Radka. She hadn't seen her in several weeks. Her normally bright yellow, silver and blue hair was fading. She was not moving. The workers spoke in hushed tones, but her memory only contained the parts of the conversation she had understood.

"...She's..."

"Gone, dissolution."

"...told to reset her unit...."

"need to bag the body..."

"extract the P_ear for the Footmen…if the grid…intact?"

"Hey, there is another User here, somewhere. Where'd she go? Rules say to wait."

"I don't see anyone."

The Baggers turned and looked where Kenda had been standing. She had hidden herself behind a delivery cutaway in the mesh of the Cretewall beside her.

"Oh, so, uhh-go ahead."

From the nook, she watched they resumed their work.

The workers looked back at the body. One of them kneeled down and pried the console out of her head. Long tendrils of wires and strands of slick root systems tethered the console to the user. Carefully cutting the wires and root tissues as close to the head as possible, Unit and User were separated. The console and its entrails were placed in a grey box. The recovery team of baggers standing by heaved the body in the bag and dragged and folded it aggressively into a transport tram bed next to three other bags. They hopped in the tram and shuttled off down a throughway.

The two remaining Baggers standing over where the body had been mused…

"another blank for the tank…"

"…that is what they say. Blank for the tank…"

"…rule one, cap the carrier, recover the cover…"

"…cap the carrier, recover the cover…like the Footmen say…it repeats again."

"Yup. Blank for the tank."

"Yup."

They went to their tram and placed Radka's boxed console into a collection bin in the back bed and rode off down a nearby throughway.

Kenda ran after them. They turned into a cut in the throughway. It had worn mesh holdings, just like Kenda's building. The cut began to seal again, after the tram sailed through. Kenda slipped inside before enclosure gate sealed again.

The inside was a cavern. Dark and dripping. Brackish shelves rose from the floor like draped skeletons. They towered, laden with pinkish burdens. The air was foul with moisture-a liquid feel-fluid sounds, oozing.

Kenda watched the tram lumber down one of the rows. The squeaking from the wheels of the tram slowly bled out.

The walls were slick with something; Kenda skittered away from them. She moved toward the greyblack shelves. Their bony bleak sides and their pinkish cargo rattled her. She was close enough to see now, but she still didn't comprehend. There was stuff in front of her, pink-greyish masses that filled row after row, blobs that almost seemed to pulse. She touched one and it sang under her fingers, throbbing with her own heart, but clinically, mechanically. She lifted it up from its tray. Long tendrils swung from the underside.

She thought, "*The P_ear consoles-storage-.*" A clank sounded behind her. She crept over to the last row and peered around. She was face to face with a moving belt. Whizzing past her were P_ear units. She could see the slick pink innards trailing behind each one.

One more door. In the passway to her left. It was open, and she ducked through. She came face to face with something she had no words for. Human forms were stacked floor to ceiling. Yellow lights shone behind their eyes. They were connected by slick, braided cords that glowed. The lights and the glowing braids thrummed and flickered. She felt an electrical presence. The air cracked and popped with it. The tower undulated. Somewhere deep inside her, she did not believe what she was seeing. She wanted to break the dream's hold, to unsee it. Purging was not enough; she had to physically disprove this thing.

She touched the shoulder of the nearest body. Microtendrils wound around her wrist. A pop exploded in her head. Pushed data streams raced through her mindscreen –*Ceramicats make the best pets—user 4523Avainon says that it decreases kanker—Shugso and*

Thinbanana can pair for a fun drink!—purrsonality gives you happy points----Skinshine makes the scars fade faster-guaranteeeeeeeeeeeed--

The messages came faster, tumbling and roaring like a tide. She couldn't keep them separated. She heard several error messages sound off in her head to assimilate and relay the messages through the network. She tore at the tendrils on her wrist; they had tightened and organic binders had already seeped into and were burrowing into her skin. She scratched, caged rat for survival-blood flew from the open wound. She pulled away throwing herself backwards. Heads from around the room tilted her way, unblinking eyes glowed orange, then faded to yellow. The breach she created sealed itself. Heads reset their erect posture, and their eyes flickered and the network glowed back into its pulse to life again. She ran from the room with a wordless scream caught in her throat.

🐾 Cats through the Looking Glass

Kenda shook the memory from her head. When she could look at RiEF again, she spoke, "I haven't thought of that for a long time. The bodies. The network. All that data must be passing through them, like through them-broadcast?"

RiEF nodded. "That seems likely. You are the first to have verified that. Others have reported it, but only as others have told them. You are the first to source that information." RiEF shivered and paused the recording; DNA strands stopped falling in the tube.

"I know how hard this is for you-such horror. This is monstrosity. Never think that my duties to record interfere with how my heart sears for you. All that you have been through-someday it may help for others to know. I believe this. This is why Spine exist. Sometimes it helps to access the right words. To listen to the conversations of time. The heartbeat of humanity. The thoughtful tide. The song of centuries."

"Thanks, RiEF," Tears dipped and rolled over Kenda's scarred cheeks. She wipes them away, "Horror fits-monstrosity, yes, but inhumanity? That word keeps coming up to me when I try to place it. I agree that sourcing it is the first step. You are right. Thank you. We are nothing without a living record."

RiEF smiled. "That's what we are. Living records. Let's take a break. Walk down to dinner, and meet me later. XY will morg me if I wear you out."

❧ Chapter on Insurance

"Culture doesn't evolve, because that suggests a linear pattern, yet it builds and transforms behind itself not only what it is building, while it is building it, it retools its own process for building. It is an exponentially expanding geodesic of transmission and reception funneled again through complex networks only to be re-released moments later." Jernull Banburn, *Tangential Theorems Thesis, revised after the First Gathering.*

Jernull, who was still reeling from the kiss, wandered around the *Coolwalk!* in the direction of his Paternal figure's office. He'd been trying to apply what he had discovered about interest and insurance to the events that almost got him kicked out of school. It had been a while since he had thought of the incident. He had been asked to direct a Billy story. The Billy Story Theater is a series of Vidcasted playlets sponsored currently by *SympaticoCouch-the couch that feels with you!* It had taken him a while to get the story right and produce the audio/vids, but he had been fairly pleased with the result. He was not happy with the viewer response.

After the first vidCast, he had paced the broadcast bank fretfully. The Billy story had concluded for the 1:48 p.m. vidCasts request group. He was waiting for the applause response relays that didn't come from an audience who wasn't there. The Billy story play, entitled, <u>Beat Down</u> was sent as vidCasts streamed to their P_ear consoles. As the vidCasts concluded, there was very little response, but what of it there was, was negative. Billy Stories are big credit generators, and he was failing to make any. He pulled up the responses in his mindscreen…

CHIRPREVIEWS RECEIVED FOR <u>BEAT DOWN</u>=3700/4.5 million viewers, complete listing of CHIRPS:

--USER:CULLYDUD78943: Borings! Where are the ThinBananas in this story?

-- USER:DRONEBID452398: I know, right? I don't even know what was the runner was doing-why didn't they surrender to the walking people?

Jernull stopped collecting the Chirps. He moved his hands over the broadcast panels and began to send the vidCasts out to the 2:00 p.m. request viewers, hoping there was someone out there that would understand.

In order to avoid his Paternal figure's wrath, he decided it was best not to mention the Footmen, or the Spine for that matter. He knew interest was at work in that decision. Even though he actually had seen the Spine being beaten by the Footmen, but the Footmen worked with his Paternal figure's company, and he knew that would cause problems, at least he thought it would-he just didn't know why. So, he had decided to represent each with something else, of his own making, giving a new name and different attributes for each involved player to avoid problems. He called the Footmen, the Walking Men and the Spine were called Runners. It was, as he put it, 'insurance against doing nothing' to quell the protest in his heart at seeing the beating in real life.

He sent out the broadcast again to the 2:00pm viewers.

BEAT DOWN-A BILLY STORY

Produced by Jernull Banburn

Brought to you by

SympaticoCouch-

the Couch that feels with you!

Narration: Late last night, something happened. A woman was heard shouting in the street...

Side note: Scenery includes some areas and some things. Descriptions of people are what you might expect.

Runner: There is only fear in darkness.

Walking Man: Hold there, keep quiet. You are not authorized to be here.

Runner: Why not?

Walking Man: Because what you are saying is—is—dangerous.

Runner: Dangerous to whom?

Walking Man: It is upsetting people-the shouting. The words disturb the calm of the streets.

Runner: Words are understanding.

(The Walking Man hits the Runner in her knees. She sinks to the ground. Several hits bring her to the floor.)

Runner: There is fear in darkness. Disintegration brings the light.

Narration: The woman slips away into the CarnivalDusk Funlight. The Walking Man goes home. When he sits in his new *SympaticoCouch*, he forgets all about the Runner.

Thank you for watching! Remember to buy your new emotional best friend today-the *SympaticoCouch!-the couch that feels with you!*

It cradles, coddles all your naps,

Emotional comfort in a snap!

*****THE END*****

Thank you for watching our VidCast of <u>BEAT DOWN.</u> Chirppreviews will be accepted for the next 30 seconds.

He set the broadcasts to automatic-at 10 minute intervals. The play was not well reviewed in the next round of chirps by the vidCast audience either. There was a single reviewer that seemed to understand some piece of Jernull's play.

Ambiashin784: I felt bad for the Runner. That play is [system unable to transcribe this word, please try again]something.

One User. A single entry among a sea of indifference. That wasn't enough. Not nearly. Jernull chewed the inside of his cheek. He shoved his bangs out of his eyes and stormed out of the building. He walked briskly, but aimlessly, wading through the standard fare of littered labels, away from the campus. There was no one on the streets due to a pending light rainfall.

Jernull pulled himself out of the memory of that disastrous day. He grabbed his forehead and rubbed, the memory was painful, but instructive. If this incident taught him anything, it was that even though there must be more stories out there that he needed to tell, he was afraid that very few cared to hear them. *"No, that's not it. Maybe there are those that don't care. There is something else in the way of the conversation, too. What is it?"*

Jernull did not get a chance to answer himself, as he finally arrived at his Paternal figure's building. It looked unreal, as if the webbing held the Crete by the mere force of will and imagination. Like a single turn might unravel the thing.

He took the lift to his paternal figure's floor; the specific floor number was as inconsequential as the building.

🐾 Cats through the Looking Glass

During dinner, Kenda thought about how RiEF had been such a comfort to her; she had given her the gift to describe and detail what had happened and what she had seen. The gift of words. Accurate words. Like horror, tragic, amoral. Kenda felt such a rush at the understanding that could be fostered with just one word. The power not only to heal, but to spread healing exponentially. She wondered to herself during dinner, turning it over like madness, *"Why had this power disappeared? Who would be interested in numb people who were only focused on product? Who wins? Ahh. Profit is an interest. All that is left is information that doesn't cross interest lines. No substance. Purged of understanding. This is that dream of the desert mind. Slipping inside the mouth of time to speak to other ages. Even if there are story carriers; who is listening?"*

After dinner, Kenda asked if she could add another memory to the archive by herself. RiEF agreed and went with her to the recording station. She showed her how to use the machine.

"What are you recording?"

"I am going to try to archive everything that happened that day at Themall, when I met Spine and came here."

"The archive will record your memory and the emotional responses. I will be nearby in the Reference room if you need me." RiEF walked out and quietly shut the panel.

Kenda sat down at the table on RiEF's side. She was alone in the room, but she felt the warmth of purpose in her every action. She ached to make sure each word held her intent and captured the story.

Though still emotionally wrung out from relaying the story about Radka and the tower of blanks, she was determined to save every word she could remember. She switched the machine on and placed the receiver on her finger. The machine began recording the emotional effect of the tale. She thought slowly and deliberately, focusing on the details and her responses. The archive transcribed the emotional strands of the memory as Kenda recalled what happened inside Themall, just before she met her first Spine...

She had wandered as far away as she could from Dayzee and the Honeyplugs Popnchew stand. Two Footmen emerged from a corner and blocked her path near the *Maybewins Gaming Interfaces! Still only 12 credits with the possibility of winning!*

"User, you are due for another diagnostic."

"What?"

"Stop and present for additional diagnostics."

"I was just about to play a game and *Maybewin*." Kenda tapped off the mention credit, her sarcasm aside, a mention is a mention.

The Footmen grabbed her arm and forced her into a Footmen service center behind the *Maybewins* games.

"What is it now? I just had a diagnostic this morning."

"How does she know that if she was wiped?" Venz whispered through clenched teeth. His partner shoved an isolation beam under Kenda's chin and whispered in her ear, "I can isolate you right now. Stop resisting."

Kenda felt no immediate danger; at first, what she felt might easily be characterized as perplexed. It was not until she paired what Jernull's play *Beat Down*, with her current situation that she felt the cold vice of fear bear down on her.

"If they would beat Spine, they might also do something bad to me, and I cannot move."

That processing took time in her brain; it came to her consciousness gradually, like the way that the pink Funlights of dawn spread their fingertips of rose across the sky. She cast about for connections to make sense of her situation, fear fueling her rage and rage fueling rebellion.

Venz grabbed her and twisted her arm behind her back. "I think we should reboot her entire system. Go ahead and shut down hearing and memory, so we can have a look."

Kenda felt the spark of connection as the control key attempted to shut down her awareness. She collapsed from the shock into their arms, and though paralyzed, she remained aware. *"What the farce?"* she thought, *"This has meaning. This relates to all the things Jernull was trying to figure out, everything he told me. What reason is there for them to do this to me? I am getting in their way, like Jernull said. What have I been doing? Bad product reviews? Slipping on my credits…?"* Surges of pulsed sleep threatened to overtake her system. Her eyes fluttered.

Venz caught her left side as she collapsed. "Gaw! What was she doing? She was resisting a diagnostic. No one resists us, except for…Spine. She isn't responding to the retraining protocol. She has been reset every single day, twice a day sometimes. She is not supposed to remember much, but this time she remembered the exact timing of the other diagnostics."

Teves tapped his console and reported her resistance. Banburn EEMed back, "She could throw off the grid. One more bad report, and bag her."

Teves said to Venz, "Future Miss Info candidate or not, he told us she'll have to be isolated if this keeps up."

"Let's finish the check on her."

Venz got a hold of Kenda's green hair and pulled her head to the side so that Teves could get a better look at the embedded console. This stretched the skin around the unit and caused it to reopen her healing scabs and tear the healing glue patch. Blood pooled and began to clot in her hair. Kenda winced, but the two men did not notice.

Teves passed his control key by the panel again and it popped open. He gasped as he looked inside.

"Holy Farce, it looks like more growth here, I think. It's like nothing I have ever seen. There is something wrong, like…it's just so…very not the same, I mean it's wrong." He tapped in a report, hoping for guidance.

Outgoing EEM- reporting additional problems. Much larger than last time. Standing by for orders.

EEM incoming from Banburn-At this point, I need this unit to be blanked. Cap the carrier, recover the cover.

Teves' face went lax. He was glad not to have to do another diagnostic on this girl. "Banburn says to blank her. You do it. I did the last one." He threw Kenda over on her side, and her head smacked the plasmold floor. Her stomach heaved, but very little movement registered on her frozen features; the panic in her mind though, was real, *"Blank? Oh Gaw. I've got to move."* Kenda focused on pushing her limbs. They did not respond.

She managed a low grunt. Neither Footmen noticed. She moved part of her right foot. The haze was thick upon her; every part of her willed her body to motion, screamed it, but the blocking protocol was stronger than her will.

Teves strolled away from Kenda and Venz. He pressed the light button on a Staggerette-the new self-lighting Staggarette *Twobacco product! Two types of smokingjuicing for the price of 1 credit!* He smoked it and then sucked the Twobacco juice out, feeling instantly better.

"Now that's convenient Twobacco!" Credits cranked on his mindscreen. He didn't really need them, Bits and Bytes paid for anything he needed, but earning them gave him a rush.

Relieved at some patterns to follow, he tapped in a request for the Baggers to come collect the body. Then, he wandered off in a corner to play Throws for a while. He wanted to beat Garotte's high score, so he could rub it in when he saw him again.

Venz knelt next to Kenda and looked at her. Green, expressionless eyes stared back at him. Lifeless lips seemed to curve and breathe and speak. Her face in his hands seemed to radiate cold that bit his skin.

There was something edging its way around his understanding of the gravity of what he was about to do. It was a new situation for him, and he had trouble reconciling this.

He moved her hair out of the sticky mat of blood on her neck.

"Can you hear me? I have to do something to you." Venz looked around, Teves had gone out. "It's because you are broken-not working. We can't fix you. It's my turn, Teves said it is. It's just my turn, that's all. I am supposed to because he said." He made another furtive check for Venz. He tightened his grip on Kenda. Some force was compelling him forward, but there was an ache of protest that stayed him momentarily. A band of resistance was pulling taut about his resolve.

"Who are you?" Venz thought, with great difficulty. *"You don't look broken, either, like the last two."* Venz dragged his mind like a dull blade through Thin Bananas. He wanted desperately for things to fall into patterns, but this was not a repetition, this was—not a pattern.

Heroically, he thought, *"I am delivering a morg code to a functional User. There is no word for doing this. This code is not for functional Users. She does have error codes, yet she is not Push and she is not Blank. She is not Twitch."* Venz tangled within his own mind. *"I can't give a morg code to a functioning User, but I can, if Banburn requests it, give a dissolution code to a non-functioning P_ear unit."*

He sat back on his heels, satisfied. "I can do that."

He frowned. "That will morg the body, though. The body that is functional." He rolled his eyes. *"But if I fail to carry out an order from Banburn-I lose my job."*

This fleeting moment was a bit of a promise for all humanity, a promise made to the unborn, the young, the vulnerable, that panthers might not feast. All that in one small burst of hope at its most stark-raving mad.

However, in a justification as old as most wars, Venz weighed, what Jernull would call interest, and found a rationale he could live with.

He reset his shoulders, lingered no more, and made a motion across the sensors to initiate

.:.*dissolution*.:.

This meant fading out, ending. The shutdown began. Kenda's eyes fluttered. Her P_ear light signaled alternating green and black, as the code began running.

Behind him, there was a shriek and Teves' body dropped in through the door pocket of the adjoining room, collapsing on the floor with a sickening crunch of bones, dead before he hit the ground, presumably from the bootprint that had caved in his chest, stopping his heart. A woman, wearing a pair of stolen Footmen steel-soled shoes, stepped through the door frame.

Kenda's eyes struggled to open, her neck tensed as she tried to turn her head. She could not make out what was happening. She could see shades of another person moving around the room. The codes set in motion were burrowing into her psyche, but she tried to keep her focus. Her mindscreen lit up with lines of code. The room was spinning, her mindscreen flashing warnings, "Override user protection protocol? *Denied*...Override morg codes?-----*Denied*. Continue with systems shutdown? *Resuming*...Matrices failing....failing...////"

She heard another yelp, this time it had been from Venz, followed by a single loud crack as his head split open at the intersection where his silver P_ear console met his real ear. It appeared to be dented with a heavy object in the shape of a semi-circle, again-the exact shape of the powerful- plated boot. There was a swish of a long black cloth that settled on Kenda's shoulder. Soft hands smoothed Kenda's cheek and coursed effortlessly around the P_ear console. Kenda focused on her internal mind screen and saw the lethal words:

...Beginning .:Dissolution:. Protocol...

She thought, *"Total erasure? I will be a blank. I am going to Morg."* She couldn't move to stop the code. She tried desperately to manipulate her mindscreen. She couldn't see the other person's face; her paralysis was fading, but not fast enough. The hands of the unknown person worked on Kenda's console furiously, tapping like a whisper. The program code for .:dissolution:. had disappeared from her mindscreen and it was being replaced with a code Kenda knew from many other diagnostics that she could remember clearly.

It was a wake up code.\\\Systems Reboot///

The gentle hand smoothed her hair, carefully snaking the green locks around her ear-manually. Something cold was applied to her wounds. She began to feel again. Her internal readout flashed in her head ...*system check*...*Emotional Transfer Grid inoperable*...*all console other matrices normal*... *system returned to user control*...*limited network access, inflow only*/////

Kenda's eyes snapped open. She heard a Footmen alarm from the P_ear units that the Footmen wore, "THIS IS NOT ROUTINE. STAY STILL. DO NOTHING. MORE FOOTMEN ARE COMING TO HELP YOU." As an added bonus, another announcement also sounded in and outside her head, *"Please sit still. Your diagnostic is not complete. Footmen have been dispatched to help you. Stay very still. You may damage components by attempting to move. This will void your warranty and cost many credits to repair. Thank you for using the P_ear Network. We work hard to keep you as a user."* Another voice sounded, very near her ear. A real voice in the physical world whispered to her, "If I am not back in two minutes, I'll meet you at your apartment. I've set your console timer. Don't forget. They will be back. I am going to get more help. We only have 14 minutes before the nearest Footmen arrive." Soft hands pulled her to a seated position. A moment later, she caught a glimpse of the long, black coat, retreating out the door panel. She rubbed her head with the back of her left palm. She grabbed onto the metal shelf to her right and pulled up.

The world swam into focus like a wave.

She looked at the Footmen on the floor. She recalled the ads, *"Has an LED indicator has gone from green to black? EEM an alert to DeadBags-WE zip and ship for free. Report all LED dead lights to Bits and Bytes! And you keep the 120 credit P_ear recovery fee!"* The two Footmen had black indicators. Dead. Morg. Stillness and dead, pairing. Not-speaking and dead. Pairing. She reached down and touched the face of the man nearest her. She felt his smooth cheek. She felt gripped by something. She wondered at the way her stomach clenched. She wished for a word to describe it. What does that mean? The warning timer that the stranger had set for two minutes blared on her console. She tapped it off. She remembered the other thing that the woman had said, "Kenda, don't forget two mintues- run. Meet me at your building---"

Another alarm sounded in her head, but this time, it was deafening. Her face shook with it, ***"FOOTMEN HAVE BEEN DISPATCHED..."***

She slapped off the external speaker and shook away the internal warning on her mindscreen.

She got up to leave. From the door panel of the Footmen Control Center, she saw Themall nearly empty. Slipping out, she hurried down the Coolwalk! toward her apartment. Her balance wasn't quite recovered; she was still rebooting, so she slapped credits off to reset the Coolwalk! to a fast- moving viscosity. The Blowers on the Coolwalk! blew the wrappers and trash out of her way and drained a preset amount of credits, for this service. She stopped doing that halfway there because she thought they may be able to see her purchases and her location. The voice that saved her had told her to go to her apartment. She had to trust that voice. It belonged to the person had reversed the morg codes.

Without the Blowers, she kept tripping on the piled wrappers and cream bowls. *"This is a trash world."* The pairings were coming easier for her. *Morg." Kenda muttered, as she tottered, ran headlong, "Dead and not speaking, dead and still,"*

"The dead do not speak, they do not move, so life is paired to movement and speaking. I move. I use words. I am not dead. The Footmen were trying to make me dead. They put an isolation beam under my chin. They had entered a .:Dissolution:. code in my console. Interest and insurance. I AM NOT DEAD. I move. But. But. I do stand at charging walls for hours. I speak. I SPEAK. What did I have to say? Other people's words. I only paired other people's words. Am I dead?" She touched her console again and felt the warm pulse of her LED, this did little to reassure her that she was alive. She stepped off the Coolwalk!, staggered through knee-high product casings and labels and nearly folded herself into her apartment building. She wondered about the implications of that word, *"Meant to be apart. People are not meant to be apart."*

She stepped off the lift and into her room. The door panel slid closed behind her. She held her hand to EEM something to someone about what had just happened.

Her thoughts were thrashing about, *"Someone saved me. Who was it? It would make a great newsport, but like Jernull's play would anyone report it? Would anyone want to hear it? My dreams. Nobody to give my story to. Desert minds."*

She didn't know whom to EEM; Jernull would likely not respond and no one else would understand. Plus, the Footmen monitored all EEM traffic. *"They would have an interest in finding me because they want to blank me. The alarm said it was a mistake, but it wasn't; that Footmen had set a morg code."* She sloughed through the wrappers on her floor, trying to clear her head, her words mirroring the sound, *"Trash, trash, trash world."*

Her ceramic cat tinkered over to her, tripping on the wrappers, softly emitting its mechanical purr. She picked it up and the purring got louder, more akin to a whirr now though, fighting to push through damaged gears. Funlight filtered through the broken blinds, sending forth its steady and awkward artificial light that settled on the CeramiCat's face, and its broken, suddenly illuminated muzzle scared Kenda.

She took a good steady look at her Ceramicat. Bleary-eyed from the reset and the run back, she took as close an inventory as she was able to. The light showed the true contour of the automaton's poorly formed mouth, which was jaggedly painted into a semblance of a smile. Metal and wires hung out, suggestive of spilling innards, from broken ceramic panels on its sides, and its tail had long since fallen off. Inside of the ceramic cat, something sparked and twitched within the bulging wired frame.

Kenda searched her head for a pairing, *"Ceramicat and broken, CeramiCat and morg; it already was morged? This thing could never morg, it had the appearance of living, but it is not living. This thing is not alive and it never was."*

Suddenly, she heard a woman shout from outside her building. She concentrated on the *Winraise-We open your window blinds, don't lift a finger, and think your window blinds open!* She tried to think the blinds open, but they wouldn't open. Then she remembered. They weren't working. She would need to engage it, physically. She rushed over and manually pushed the panel up. Through the Lookingglass Window Pane, she saw a woman being clubbed repeatedly by two Footmen with the short grey Snapstix attachment on their Heart and Mind Iso Beams. The woman crouched and blocked the blows. She struggled to get up.

Kenda thought that the woman had on the same long black cloak that she had seen when the diagnostic went wrong. "It must be her." She couldn't be sure, rebooting affected all the senses. Right at this moment, she couldn't even be sure of her own existence.

This whole thing looked like the beating Jernull had described in his play. Kenda had never seen anyone being beaten and did not know if she should send an EEM to the Footmen, for how could she call Footmen to report on the Footmen? That made no sense. She looked around at the other buildings. All the other windows were cloaked with Winraise blinds, but hers. No one else had them opened and no one was on the street because of the scheduled rainfall that had not materialized yet. Grey hazed from the Footmen-activated Funlights. Kenda looked down at the woman again.

Her long hair was dark brown, from the nursree rhymes. Cutichrome and overlays had been the fashion for so long; no one would be caught dead going natch and even if they did, it would be an altered natch, like blond or orange, with streaks of brown. This woman was clearly natch. No brandsponsor owned her. This woman was clearly Spine.

The woman slumped forward, and the Footmen shoved her down on the Coolwalk! so hard it triggered an audio advertisement to blare out-"*Coolwalk! A Resin-composite cushion cooled walkway!- Turn it up or down for hard or soft walking modes, we walk-with you not against you-use your control credits today!! Now with Blower Trash Removal breeze, only .34 credits more per mile!*"

The boots of the Footmen had automatically hardened the Coolwalk! surface. The woman's forehead struck it with a snick noise. Blood wept from her temple. The Footmen grabbed her ankle and struggled to keep her still. Kenda felt a rawness build within her-a rage- if she had known that word- it would have fit. Her hands closed on her palms pressing tight and drawing up. Her eyes narrowed. She thought, *Why is this happening? None of the Newsporters tell us this. Jernull was right, his Billy story was right, people should know this, but they don't know it, maybe no one would hear it, but I am looking at it and I know it, though. I could vidcast it or I could…"*

Kenda pressed her hands against the Lookingglass panel and pushed it hard until she felt the Placeless bend and crack, sending feathers of Placeless in an arc that wafted harmlessly away on the breeze. The evening air rushed in and closed over her.

Now, she finally had a clear, unobstructed view.

Inside her head a warning sounded, "*….you may be voiding your window warranty…-*". Kenda slapped it away and looked down at the scene below. The quiet disintegration of the Placeless had not interrupted the Footmen in their task.

The taller one tried to hold the woman down with his knee in her back. He yelled, "Check her ankle Juffv. That's where the Tatter gun marks are-"

"Farce you, banger-I'm trying. You could give me a hand-It's there! She is probably the one who just applied the dissolution protocol to Teves and Venz."

"Gaw. Dissolution protocol, Vex that, she kicked a chest in and broke a skull. With our boots. It repeats again."

"I don't think this has ever repeated."

The two men froze. The fact that they couldn't use their words of comfort was highly uncomfortable. They only knew how to respond to predictable events using simple outcomes. They got paid for maintaining repetition, putting people and units back on the same path or to call for a zip and ship.

The Spine woman tried to push them off her. They clapped her hands with beam cuffs and drove her face into the Coolwalk! again where her head dragged a great smooch in the surface. Without realizing it, Kenda clenched her fists so tightly, her nails cut ten fine moon-shaped arcs in her palm. A fire was building within her. A floodgate threatened to buckle.

The woman lay motionless on the *Coolwalk!* The two Footmen stood over her, huffing out deep breaths of air, both of their hands were on their knees. Juffv took out his isolation beam and pointed it at the woman's head.

Kenda sucked in her breath. She picked up her *Ceramicat-the friendly cat you don't have to feed!*

She yelled out the window frame, "Stop that!" and heaved the *CeramiCat at them.* It meow-ed the whole way down to finish with an ear-splitting caterwaul as it smashed on the hardened Coolwalk!.

"Your Ceramicat warranty is void. Throwing the cat is not a suggested use for Ceramic---"

The crash startled the two Footmen who ducked the fragments flying toward them. Juffv leaped backward and in doing so, accidentally discharged his weapon into the *Coolwalk!* rendering its controls temporarily disabled and causing it to reset into *Marshmellowmode for heavy walkers-easy breezy, good for the knees!* Both Footmen lost their balance and began trying to grab each other for stability. They slapped at their control units and stomped their boots trying desperately to reset the *Coolwalk!*

Kenda took the lift down and ran out of her building to confront the Footmen. Juffv had regained his stance and raised his weapon to the woman laying quite still on the walkway.

Juffv's partner, Garotte, shouted "Don't move." as he pointed his own weapon at Kenda, emerging from her apartment doorframe.

"What are you doing?" she shouted.

"This woman is a crimeoffender of the highest order. We are going to take her in to be processed."

"I know you. You rebooted my P_ear this morning."

Teves dug into his pocket and pulled out a small square control key on a chain which he dangled in front of Kenda and said, "We can do it again, right here. Help you forget."

"Looks to me like you are going to isolate this woman." Kenda felt a boldness running through her as she spoke these words-a surge, like when Jernull talked about interest and insurance, passion. She realized right at this crucial moment that she liked that feeling; it felt right. She had questions. She knew the men were lying. It was clear they were trying to isolate this woman. Their weapons were set with the stunner in the off position, one pulse and she'd never have a chance. This was an M-42 Heart and Mind Isolation Beam that they were holding. But, she had no time to ask any more questions.

Answers came swiftly from the woman on the ground. She suddenly sprang into animation, doing a lethal back kick into Juffv's midsection with boots that had steel soles; his face turned a hazy shade of purple as he dropped neatly to the *Coolwalk!*, groaning. His tongue lolled out slick with his own blood. The woman rolled over and kicked Garotte, dropping his legs out from under him, which due to his considerable girth, caused at least one of his knee joints to rip out sideways and he collapsed, writhing in agony, next to the now motionless Juffv.

The woman hopped to her feet and ran on the slowly congealing Coolwalk, which had rebooted and just reached MEDVIS or *Medium Viscosity for light to moderate runners!* level. It made for slow going, and the woman was bleeding badly, but she managed to make it over to Kenda who said to her, "You're bleeding badly."

"I know," the woman replied, "but, more Footmen are coming and they are going to isolate us both, we've got to go."

Kenda felt a new sense of fear and something else, something tightening her stomach. She bounced on the squishy Coolwalk! to get her footing and ran after the woman trying to keep up. The woman slapped at her own set of Footman boots which reset the *Coolwalk!*

An announcement sounded from a nearby console:

"Viscosity change confirmed! *Coolwalk!* Your setting is *[firm] Use firm for speed-when you have to go-go-go!* "

They ran for a long time until they reached a throughway, which serves as an access passageway between buildings used by loading vessels. The woman drew an interrupter from a side pocket and dispatched with the beam cuffs. She was breathing heavily. She changed a setting on the interuptor and it on her wound.

Kenda tore a piece of her sleeve and did her best to wipe the woman's wound clean, it was streaked with blood. She looked for something to hide them and saw a large loading bay doorpanel. She and the woman pushed into the door frame and they both disappeared from the street view.

She had barely sat down, when the woman stirred abruptly and whispered, "Source!" She leaned down and held Kenda's ankle. She stabbed it with her interrupter, which Kenda realized was not a true interrupter but some modded-out version that bore a resemblance to a *Tattergun! Skin designs and Medical infusions made easy with Tattergun!* It bit down into the flesh of Kenda's leg just above the ankle and left hundreds of pinpricks in her skin. The marks, which quickly healed and disappeared, left behind raised glyphs on her ankle. The glyphs looked like this:

XY
401.400

The woman said drowsily, "Source flow. Carry XY." Then, she passed out on the doorpanel frame.

Tatterguns have the side effect of leaving its patients drowsy for a few minutes, and so, while the woman beside her passed out from her injuries, Kenda slipped into a semi-catatonic state, herself. Images flashed through her brain that she had never seen before.

The woman was shaking her.

"Your name? Your name?" Her voice was urgent and worried.

Kenda replied through a sluggish voice "I…cause.. whyy…uh…" and then more clearly "Kenda."

"Kenda, good, you sourced XY well. The Footmen will find us. We need to move. Can you walk?"

"Yes, I—"

"Good, let's go this way." The woman pointed, Kenda could barely make it out, a small bright spot at the end of the throughway.

Footsteps sounded behind them, followed by predictable shouting and a scuffle to get into the dimly lit throughway. Kenda leaned against the Cretemixed wall for balance, her fingers poked through the wall support mesh and curled around it. She flexed her fingers and poked deeper until she managed all the way through the hexagonal webbing. Her fingers reconnect with her palm, forming a circle. She felt a surge of energy as a rush of new words and their meanings flooded her mind-pictures of architectural design patterned after the ones she leaned against; ornate and simple lines, spires, arches, balance, ballast, foundations, gravity. She tugged the web, she pulled and popped a main seam of the webbing and it ran to the roof of the building out of her sight. Chunks tumbled, sending a scree of Cretemixed fragments exploding from all sides. The building groaned and screamed, its viscera collapsing out of it. Kenda ran, leaving the grey-black building to wash its straits into the throughway and cover their escape.

She sprinted after the woman. The path behind her closed shut; the world was swimming before her. This dizziness was symptomatic of Tattergun aftereffects, but there was an undercurrent of some type of new knowledge streaming through her mind that muddled it. She had no time to assimilate or make sense of it; she ran headlong to keep up with the woman in front of her.

They kept to the throughway and burst forth into the brightness, some color of SolarFlair light that Kenda had never seen, and she did not fully understand its intensity, for she was hurtling headstrong at a speed that threatened to spurn her to the ground at any moment. They swam up main streets only to dart down more throughways and connectors, until they came to a black lacquered resin door.

The woman next to her, rapped quickly on the doorpanel, even though there was an *Eliass Family Entry Button* right on the side of the doorpanel. The door slid open into a doorframe pocket and the woman jerked Kenda inside the darkness on the other side of the threshold. As the door slid sideways into the panel, Kenda was astonished to read letters on the crux under the door. It said, "Rue Beacon." Her heart thrilled, "*Letters in the physical world.*"

The lights slowly raised in the hall where they were standing. Kenda looked at the woman she'd followed after they'd caught their breath and sputtered, "What the farce is going on?"

Two brown-haired women entered the hall and began to inspect the wounds of the Spine woman who waved them off, saying, "Not now. I'll be fine for now. They struck at Themall. Tram was at the apartment, but it was gone when we got back there. I had to do a field source. She managed a wall to cover our escape. Pulled a main seam, I tell you! Assimilated the language of architectural structures, she's... she's been Sourced, maybe correctly. Let's get her down to the stackroom."

Turning to Kenda, she said, "Please, just trust me a little longer. You must be feeling that I mean you no harm by now."

"Yes, but I have so many questions."

"I will do my best to answer them."

"Just one, first."

"Ask. Never let it be said I turned down a query." The two women waiting next to them smiled and relaxed a bit.

"So, you are Spine?"

"Yes. Are you frightened? Beware the brown hair and all that?"

"No. I-think-well-you saved my life. What is your user id? Mine's Harkonna311371." Kenda felt silly after the words left her mouth, obviously this woman had no P_earnet access, she had no P_ear console embedded in the side of her head, nor one on her wrist.

"I am not a user on the P_earnet. But, as for my name, I am called XY."

Kenda attempted to pronounce the name herself, "Kes' why?"

"Yes, exactly. It is spelled X-Y." She lifted up her ankle and showed the glyphs scarred into the tissue. "These are my Calling numbers. I was called to serve the Spine in a similar way as you were, my anger brought me here."

"Those are the same marks you put on me!" Kenda said, suddenly recalling the Tattergun, looking down at her ankle, where blood congealed around the very same raised glyphs.

"It was my gift to you- you saved my life. It is a great honor to serve Source and I hope you will feel the same. Come."

"One last thing."

XY nodded.

"*Did* you save me at Themall-reset the morg code?"

XY nodded and with great reverence, did a curious sign over a scar under her left eye. "I was sent by Spine to retrieve you; we call that a minding mission. We had reasons to believe that the diagnostics were going to kill you or that the Footmen would simply install the .:Morg:. program. Most times we are too late or we can't get access without being vidcasted. The Footmen had inspected and reinstalled your P_ear programming several times in the last two weeks and your behavior had not changed. Each time they reported the problem was getting worse. They felt the network was being compromised; they meant to isolate you. When I set your system to reset, I knew you needed time to recover, and I had to arrange our exit tram to outrun the city's Footmen. I told you to meet me at your apartment. The tram was gone, ABie was driving it. Good to see she's fine." She nodded to one of the women there.

"The Footmen pursued me on a chase through the streets for a long time, when I lost them, I came back, but you were gone. I am so sorry."

XY put her hand on ABie's shoulder, "It just went wrong-the misleading reports by the Footmen have been throwing us off lately. There will be time to recap later, let's get her down to the stacks."

Kenda followed the three women up a hall and then down a long set of graduated steps that led into a wide lit room. A single chair and table were the only things in the room. The women helped her into the chair.

"We have taken the first steps of indoctrinating you by injecting you with Source Material 401.400. Your primary is language, but you have every other piece, too. This next step requires a leap of faith from you, but we need to do it before we show you anything else, not to do so would jeopardize our lives and mission."

"I am ready. I think I am anyway. What is it?"

"We are going to remove your P_ear console."

"I thought that couldn't be done! Really bad things happen-I mean, brain hemorrhage or balding or Comatoes or..."

"It has never happened, we have performed thousands, some even back when our technology and the P_ears were more primitive. RiEF here, she's had it done, with a similar unit to yours. Show her RiEF."

The woman named RiEF pulled back her hair to reveal faint pink scars.

"How do you know about me?"

"We monitor P_ear transmissions, scouting for lives to save, new Spine to recruit. The Footmen are mentally lazy, they don't put the right codes in, so we don't know the severity, except for the repetitions of upgrades and diagnostics on a User. I think the Footmen are getting ahead of our steps; they were coming for you, when I intervened. They seemed to know where we are going to be on the last few recruits and have beaten or met us there."

"Why did you pick me?"

"We use something to filter and find daily messages that are anomalies, things that indicate you'd be amendable to what we do. We look for marked changes; you have gotten more angry and frustrated with the constant advertisements, you shut down end of day summaries regularly and you've had an inordinate amount of upgrades and diagnostics in the past month. We knew we could help you, if you wanted to join us."

"We always have a strong feeling about the people we choose and we usually don't do field sourcing, but I thought I was dying and I didn't want to leave the loaded Tattergun in the field, so we are in an odd position. That code, which is now written into your DNA, is an organic manifestation of information. When you assimilate that knowledge, you might feel the full web in which we are all a part. You will be connected to Source. The human conversation, long silent, still whispers, even now. It has already spoken to you, long before we came. You turned from the world you know and reached toward the deep end, instead of drawing back to the shallows."

Kenda ran her fingers over the scars on her face, "Will I be able to know what you know?"

"Yes, all we can give you."

"Will I be able to see Jernull again?"

"Only time and circumstance will tell, but it may not be wise. He is the selected-progeny-heir of a powerful entity that has an interest in our suppression and destruction."

Kenda hesitated. She touched the console that had been her lifeline to the world. That wasn't right. It had been her world. For a while now, though, the world had ceased to make sense to her. These women offered the chance to make sense, or at least, learn about another side of it.

After a while, Kenda asked, "Do you know about interest?"

XY smiled and nodded her head, "I will make that your first lesson, if you like."

Kenda nodded, "I'll do it."

XY took a silver paddle from the glowing box on the table and put it next to Kenda's P_ear.

On a screen in the floor, Kenda read…initializing removal …disconnect neural grid…grid dysfunctional or grid not found…neural tissue connection not found…discard jumped memories…complete…erase hidden VirtuOso files…Adjacker files quarantined…shutting down power sources...P_ear disconnected---

The women worked swiftly and Kenda felt a strange sensation, as the unit was being separated from her. She felt Source, and assimilate the word, shiver, used to signify disgust or fear. Within minutes the unit was laying on the table, still glowing. XY applied white lotions to the contact openings, which dried instantly. The other two Spine women took supplies out of a cubby and dressed and cleaned Kenda's wounds and tended to XY's wounds. They gave both of them medicines to swallow and brewed a hot liquid to drink. XY nodded to the two women and they left the room.

XY picked up the console and handed it to Kenda who looked at it. She slid her finger around the interface panel, feeling the curved sensors that her fingers once flew over. She tried mentally to open the familiar mental screen in her head and nothing appeared. There was only quiet.

She handed the unit over to XY. "I don't want it."

XY smiled and dropped the unit to the floor. "They sometimes keep transmitting you know. Even though they are wiped and disconnected from you-they will sometimes keep transmitting for 2 weeks all external noises and voices, when they are deactivated or removed. That was how some of the first Spine were infiltrated-they barely made it out with the Source intact. But we learned."

"So how do you stop it from transmitting?"

XY smiled and dropped the unit on the floor. She crushed it under her grey-black boot heel-a Footmen boot. A high-pitched squeal emanated from the thing and it abruptly slowed to a whine and then faded out. A glowing sickly yellow light blinked feebly several times and at last flickered to black, then off completely.

"Now, it is morg."

"Morg? It is not living; it cannot morg."

"It was semi-organic."

"Semi-organic?"

XY nodded, her face darkened, and all of her business and solemnity returned. "We discovered that the technology relies on a partial external neural component within the implant, responsible for the machine's organic bonding, translations and transmission, using the brain's own electrical impulses. Grown neural tissues are added into all electronic P_ears to assist emotional transfer on a grid that is fed through an organic network. The tendrils-you can see them right there. This tissue has the sole purpose of enhancing and augmenting ads and newsports, with added emotion, making them more attractive to the sender and thereby transferring that emotion to the end-user. They also work in concert with emotional furniture like SympaticoCouch. The other thing that the P_ear units provide is something that used to be called access. The ultimate means of getting to something-a direct line-in to end user from sender. Ads were put directly onto things. This was before the digital divide, the cataclysm. But, now inside the mind, the very screen of the mind-the emotion and the access spurs users into consumption."

"How can they get me to do all that?"

"The neural connection in the P_ear-it is living tissue that works through your Emotional Transfer Grid, juiced emotion, but your grid had a leak and, and over time, it has been rendered null."

"Tissue from where?"

"From Twitched senders, the Push, and Blanks."

"I've seen something like that. Not the bag and ship, but the usage of tissue for the network."

"Human neural tissue, harvested from blanks, proved far better at provoking emotional responses and mimicking the electrical paths of thought than a synthetic neural system. It also has the potential to form bonds with host tissues."

Kenda tilted her head and looked upward. A word came to her. "Insidious. That is---I have nothing to pair that with that-"

XY turned her face away from Kenda and said quietly, "Truly, it is unspeakable. Well said. They need emotional responses to sell things, but there was a period of grave de-sensitivity wherein ads ceased to work. Except for the most extreme levels. People were no longer susceptible to the commercial interests that bombarded them. After the cataclysm, one company devised the first generation of consumer credits paid for by advertisers and issued free communication devices-the first gen of wrist P_ear was born. They still couldn't get people to buy products at the rate to recoup losses-so they devised the implant which linked user brains to ads and this evolved to provide the best solution."

"Let me give you some archival background from Source, this is leading up to the causes of the cataclysm." She gave Kenda a set of semi-circular cushioned wired devices and helped Kenda put them over her ears. Then she pressed a button and spoke into the table, "Can you come back in and set the recordings for Kenda?"

The two women, who had helped them down here re-entered. One of them queued up a recording with the dials on the wall and said, "This is one of the ones we only have the audio of, it all started with debate over the archives…." She pressed a triangle button and a crackle came through the rough speaker…Seenennenn brings you complete coverage of the Archive project debate….Right now we go live to the Senit hearings with our own Judd Miswah….Judd…Right Ken, today during the morning session, the leaders of a group called Consorcium testified about the need for oversight and tighter controls on the information architecture. They were citing the problems inherent in an algorithm-based-computer-controlled decision-making-process, called ABCC-DMP….Whoa, slow down there Judd, can you chew that mouthful down to a bite size for us here?…Sure, Ken….basically the group doesn't like the way the stuff is saved in the Digital Archives, they say it's arbitrary or can lead to arbitrary decisions about what is kept versus what is bumped….Judd, what is bumping? Can you break that down for our viewers at home?…Sure, Ken… What is crucial to this part of the debate and the most important aspect about the process is the protocol by which the algorithm filters out bad-or outdated informat---Sorry to cut you off Judd, we will get back to you later…We have to go now, live, to the front of the Capitol building where Candy Lane, the lead singer of Immaculate Orcasm is hand delivering her GOLD AND BOLD recordings to the Digital Universal Management Project, and we know that's a beat that won't get bumped! I give you over to Seenennenn's own, Bali Senderson who is standing next to Kayne Abull, who is Candy Lane's infamous bodyguard and on again-off again fiancé…"

"Kenda, here is one a little later in the timeline." The taller woman pushed another button, and another voice boomed inside the cushioned devices over Kenda's ears, "...we need visionaries on this project, so as Chair of the Digital Archive Project, I had agreed to sit down with the Consourcium people and the Association of News Agencies and even the group Info Watchdog. But I have taken that off the table because of their recent *un*-civil disobedience had turned up the heat on us. I am making a motion this week to table that effort and simply move forward without their input...."

Another button, more voices, almost a choir of voices, "...Mr. Speaker, Senitors I have formally requested that Info Watchdog be put on both the no-fly and the no-send list so that they can neither spread their lies nor access remote populations with them...We'll vote on that later Mr. Cauter, but in the meantime, have you made any progress negotiating the transfer of the {unintelligible} resources, what we have termed- the consolidation effort?....Mr. Speaker, Senitors, I have some very good news, and I've got some very distressing news. We successfully digitized most of what was deemed important, you see, that's the good news, the algorithms worked as they should and the dump protocol is in place to keep the data fresh and manageable from a cost standpoint, because if the information is important we will pay to keep it, but if it is bumped, we shouldn't charge the taxpayer to fund its storage. Now, that is all up and running. But, then there's the bad news that you may have heard this morning. These {unintelligible word} that call themselves the Consourcium have become enemies of this project meaning to sabotage it from day one, despite their pretext of a being on a purely preservation mission. As you well remember, the other side of this project was to collect and conserve all the paper hardcopies to form the consolidated {unintelligible words} rary Museum. That is to say, every book in existence, you understand, every piece of paper, every artifact we collected was sent and housed in that building. In one massive stroke, early this morning, the Consourcium, we believe, destroyed it all, my team says it was nuclear, but it may have been just some type of massive firebomb, left a greyblack fog over the area... (static) Were there any survivors? Not a one and that includes any of the known members of the Consourcium, they have vanished, nary a thumb print left behind...the area of course will be swept when we can get access to it, but it too full of dust and-"

"Sorry, that one cuts off too. This one is from the weeks following."

Kenda waited, as the recording crackled in her ears. With each one, she began to assimilate them with the information stored within her, like the inner DNA recording was activating in tandem with the one sounding in her ears. The tall woman hit another button, and a soft voice came through, "...this is terrible, this spore, detected too late cost us another forest, this time sequoias, the last remaining stand has fallen to this strain of {unintelligible}....no one can say where this will end or leave us...seeds are being saved at Svalbard, but all seeds have the same degeneration that wiped out secondary and tertiary forests. It is only a matter of time... time we are rapidly running out of...are any of us thinking how this will play out? I have my doubts that we can stop the spread put in motion by the Con---"

Kenda tried to assimilate this with the knowledge she felt within, but she was a little tired and not yet able to tap into it efficiently. She turned to XY, "What happened?"

XY looked at Kenda and then down at the table, "That is the problem. We aren't sure of the exact timeline of when the Librarians formed the Consorcium, then after the explosion, they became Spine. The explosion forced them into hiding. They were society's keepers and they continued in that role after the explosion for many generations, kept and gathered, but there is a period where there is a total darkness of material that lasted for...possibly decades. We suspect that Spine were busy surviving, mourning the loss and their role in it. No written knowledge, of any kind, from that time period has ever been found. No texts, or written documents. Documents, I will show you some presently, are pressed plant fiber surfaces inked with speech."

"All we can surmise is that the Spine was in hiding at that time, barely able to keep Source alive, let alone sort and gather. However, we do know that sometime after digitization, the scanty production of written works dwindled, even before the

Cataclysm. Then, the arboreal plague strain came and wiped it all out entirely. When creation resurfaced it was pure digital, like all things going through a process like that, the language and communication, fundamentally changed. It became something else, something that was not the stronger for it; it was diluted and sporadic. It didn't reflect human ideals and aspirations, but rather, trivia, minutia, sound bytes, newsproducts and swiping games for the wrist units."

"Long ago when Spine began the arduous process of checking it against our considerable Sources, it became clear that it was watered down and knee jerk."

"I don't-"

"Watering down is dilution, in this case spreading gifts thin so as to become bereft of all meaning and substance."

"I see."

"Knee jerk means reactionary or involuntary, in this case, always responding, never creating. A culture that began to speak with the voice of consumption, not creation. A voice that brayed at every straw on the wind and kicked up the dust of daily deeds not fit to stamp on. Dry. Arid deserts of the mind."

Kenda felt a connection. "I have dreamt of that."

"That is interesting. Seems that your mind felt it physically. Let me play another recording for you."

The unit in her ear crackled and she heard a scream,

"AHHHH-Research project due? Don't let this be you! Use only approved ABCC-DMP materials, the only ones guaranteed to find you the research paper of your dreams, like this Billy Shakespeer project-I got my project finish in half a time. Thanks DAP! This ad brought to you by the gud fokes at the Digital Archive Project."

XY continued, "As you know now, Spine are the transformation of the Consourcium Group mentioned in the audio recording, and though they hid Source after the cataclysm, they didn't destroy it. They did blow the empty tomb the Senate had built for it. But generations later, our numbers now, come from pairers, mostly. Many people see, but don't act. Others saw what was happening to me on that street and could have come to my aid, but didn't, not many ever do. It happens all the time that we are attacked and we get free by our wit, and, as you saw, our other talents. They have never taken us captive, but there is protocol when they do and it isn't pretty."

"Now, your first lesson, as you requested to know about interest. I want you to start slowly acclimating to the Source in your DNA.

Think the words, "Recall YELLOW KID".

Kenda did so.

She felt images surface in her mind of large letters and hundreds of images followed suit in rapid succession. This didn't feel like her P_ear screen of the mind. She was able to absorb the information and assimilate it.

"Unethical Journalism." She said aloud, "These were struggles in the early days of new sprint. New sprint. No, news print. That is pressed pay-per pulp with ideas on them. Paypur? Payper? Paper comes from trees—arboreal root networks were destroyed. My God. So much disintegration. Disintegration. A spraying apart, system degrading. The scope of it. Oh my god, how did I get that information?"

XY was tearing up, "You have sourced correctly; that was my same knowledge, too. There was no dilution and what's more, this time, is that I can still source it correctly, too. I think it was the faulty grid. It couldn't feed you anything, you developed your own compass."

A smaller woman with short brown hair named ABie, who was listening at the door edged in the room and said, "Are you sure, XY? Same information, no dilution?"

The two women in the room nodded. XY said to her, "I think so, I'll try it again."

"Kenda, try to source the words 'King's Coin."

Kenda did so and gave a startled oh, as the meaning assimilated into her conscious mind. Aloud she said, "A saying that makes a connection between accepting credits from a person of power, power being control, and being obligated to accept the words of that person of power, also called a ruler or a king. Put simpler, being bound by the advice of a provider."

Kenda stood up and backed away in horror, "I was...I took...upgrades... exchanged so high a price."

ABie and XY smiled, this is one they all knew.

ABie whispered, "It's a miracle, Source be cited. We have done it at last, so many years." ABie grinned and shook Kenda's hands rapidly. Her bobbed hair flopped as she bounced on her little mouse feet with as much restraint as she could manage.

"What does that mean?" Kenda asked.

The tall woman broke the restrained reverie to turn to her, "Kenda, I'm QRoSe, Head Minder, I ran several Footmen off Themall to assist your escape today. In the past, when we passed along information to our Called Spine, it came out different and most often diluted. It was hopeless, because we had to start over with each generation of acolyte retraining them on their section and others as well for the pieces that were missing. This was time-consuming, but it also took up resources and hindered our movement and progress in all other areas. We have never had a successful perfect recall, like you just showed. This is why we are so excited, we have finally gotten the encoding sequence right, and now we know that we must first isolate the faulty ETG... It may mean that we won't have to--."

"But how did I know those things. How did I learn?"

"Through the Tattergun, I copied Source to your DNA; you have XY and 401.40 to preserve, those are your primary Sources, but all the others are in there, too. But it has never worked so well before, like I said, it was always diluted or spotty, but this transfer was perfect. I think this is the sign we have been waiting for. ABie, have you finished with the diagnostic on the P_ear information we retrieved from her console?"

ABie nodded, "Like QRoSe surmised already, since that was her pet theory anyway," ABie rolling her eyes at QRoSe teasing, "It was the leak in the transfer grid, we think, that allowed her perfect assimilation. Because the external neurons never had a chance to take root and merge with her neural networks, the bond of heart and mind remained untouched, perfectly imperfected, to be tooled by her alone."

Kenda's memory faded. The rest of that day had been so joyful, but so busy and exhausting, that she did not remember much after QRoSe and ABie's revelation. She pressed stop on the recording device. She would never forget the day that XY brought her into Spine. She had wanted to record it for the archives for some time now, and she was satisfied that she had been able to add the emotional track to the information. Now that she'd put it in the archives, though, she knew that the entire Spine would access it. She smiled. That was fine by her. They were a curious bunch. Let them share in the joy that they had given her. Most of them knew the story anyway; stories travel fast in these halls, passed around, person to person.

❧ Dream

Since she had been living and working in the Spine Sanctuary, Kenda kept dreaming about gardening...

They always started the same way–in a dry field, where she could see the earth under her bare toes, where she would lean over to nudge some earth over seeds. They refused to grow. Words assaulted her, typical dream rants, turning over like the earth in her mind.

...seeds can spread and proliferate if people don't know all the story a little knowledge is dangerous a little DNA is dangerous it needs to spread and germinate seeds adapt to current climates and human needs, and if it doesn't serve to broaden the seed, then it dies, culture makes story... humans makes story to understand to metaphor humans understand through metaphor stories metaphors are stories meant to anchor in what we already know and connect to what we don't know...that comparison what story is-- a simple story and it tells us what makes sense and what is senseless... foundation of all human understanding comes down to this-story and metaphor...I know story, narrative the telling of things. But why metaphor? It is comparison. To compare is to tell a tale that is one that the listener knows to build upon..so what does that have to do with plants? Replication. DNA is a story with and without variants. Things grow to the story that they are told. Humans grow from story, change story. Spine protect source. You said once that seeds are source...Yes, true. Seeds are source for plant DNA... then story is source for human understanding.

Today, after her dream, she had an idea. She went straight down to the grow room. Everywhere she saw variation.

She recalled the dream and thought, "If Source feeds human understanding, then what is Push and Twitch?

She sat down on the dry earth of the grow room; it seemed straight out of her dream. She ran her palms over the top layer. She began sliding patterns in the grains with her fingertips. Dragging them over and back she etched wavy symbols at first. Then, she began reproducing letters she remembered from her mind screen. She smoothed over the drawing and letters and wrote her own name.

K-E-N-D-A

A hum resonated within her. A chord that sang in her own notes for the first time. She mused: me. A snapping to of senses crackled like a campfire within her.

She stared at her own name for a very long time. *Me. This is me.*

She dragged the dirt across her name. It was gone. Erased. *That is the word, yes. Gone. Twitch and Morg are erasing, damaging to the story, hiding it. Erasing part of self? Hmm, maybe. So to bring a thing into existence, we need to be active. Naming. Storytelling.*

She smoothed another flat plane and wrote out- Jernull. She traced the letters gingerly and felt an electric charge from the thought of seeing him again soon. She had to find him. Had to. They were working on it. But it was painfully slow. The things she could tell him! At the thought of talking with him about Source, interest, insurance, deserts-

She breathed deeply and did not need a couch to tell her anything.

She left the Grow room, but had no breakfast. It was part of a planned fast to prepare her for the Ceremony of the Eye today. She went out of the grow room and walked along the smooth passages to the uppermost levels. She met XY and QRoSe on the way. They both greeted her with the bent elbow, thumb and fingers extended, then curling, as they pull backward. Kenda signed the same back at them, the greeting was known throughout the Spine as "Unshelving".

"QRoSe is always the same." Kenda thought, *"She is anything but rose-like."* She loved the idea of the opposites there. Ever since she sourced the word rose and pun, she couldn't help but make that connection. QRoSe was of a formidable height, like a castle wall. She went on most minding missions, to recruit new members, mainly to head off Footmen; she was deadly with Footmen boots, on par with XY. She had a wide back and often carried new members draped over her shoulders, when they fainted. She loved to say, "A thing worth knowing, is worth a fight to keep, and knowledge reigns in a world asleep." Kenda loved that about her. Compassion and fangs in a woman whose name sounded like the word "rose".

QRoSe often did combat training with XY and ABie. RiEF stayed close to home usually didn't check out for missions, as she was not a fighter. ABie did, and was the counter to QRoSe's size, small, like RiEF, but with tiny mouse feet, small eyes and short bobbed hair that often fell in her eyes. However, ABie was fierce at defense. If attacked, she would respond with her own small fury, and she could pass unnoticed for street-level work, unlike QRoSe, whose presence was always felt and seen.

Today, though, they were headed to the ceremony. XY, ABie, QRoSe, and Kenda passed easily up a translucent green overpass to a cavernous circular room with moss floor, QRoSe, though had to duck under many of the low joists that framed the overpass.

When they arrived, a few Spine were already there, and had arranged themselves around the room, their eyes fixed on Kenda. Kenda took a seat next to the podium. When it was silent, XY stood and addressed the group.

"Welcome. Thank you for coming to bear witness. We will begin with the affirmation."

They murmured the words along with her.

Ours is but to query why
Protect, conserve, keep alive.

Never let the searching end
Always to search again.

Scar for memory of sin and sight.
Only this may make it right.

Let light burn-dance.
Wisdom exacts a price--vigilance.

The ceiling opened up and Funlight filtered in through the mesh tiles. The tiles shifted and the bland Funlight gave way to a heat that Kenda had never known. A shaft of blazing yellow light burned down through a panel covered her whole body briefly.

The light narrowed to a pulse and focused to a point on Kenda's cheek under her left eye and there burned. The panel shifted and the room was filled with the low-light again. Kenda's other scars had faded, serving as background for this new one. ABie came to her and sealed and dressed the burn. The Spine repeated the recessional.

The penance for our past mistakes-
The presence of mind for the present creates-
A witness to measure the course
Wisdom whispers with ageless remorse.
All things flow from Source.

🕮 Device and Disintegration

A few days after the ceremony, the scar under her eye had
pinkened to a smooth scar, contrasted with her dark skin.
Kenda sat in a recording room sipping a sweet, hot, aromatic
liquid that XY called brew, and Kenda had learned was akin to
an ancient drink of leaves heated in water called tea.

XY said, "The world is without metaphor."

"What's a meta for?"

'No, that's a pun."

Kenda assimilate the meaning; small waves of understanding
ebbed into her mind and lapped at the edges of her
consciousness. When she got XY's joke, she laughed. She
enjoyed wordplay and the understanding that could be drawn
from them. But she drew kind of satisfaction from
conversation. This was what it was like to talk to Jernull.

XY smiled, too. "That is some great connecting. What I
meant is that there is no more metaphor being made in the
world. The human conversation, understanding, connections,
conscious, self-awareness."

Kenda rejoined, "Conversation is talk. Everyone does it,
every day. We EEM it, speak it, and someone I know has even
smeared it on bananas." She smiled remembering Jernull's note.

"Every day words fall from lips and fade into nothing. There
are words rife with meaning, they foster understanding, rise and
gather, culminate in wisdom and solidify as monuments to the
human conversation over time and every generation gets to
understand and make them anew. For centuries, this held, until
the last gathering and the great drought of human conversation
followed, of which we have little recorded, as I said before. After
the dark time, the words that continued are those that fall dead
the moment they are uttered, they give nothing to eternity."

"How do those other words come about? The important
words. Where do they come from?"

"Meditation. Discourse. Many voices over thousands of
years, speaking up, turning over thoughts upon the millions like

seeds into the earth. Each generation sowing its own into the earth of their past, growing some vines, abandoning others, spurred on by replications that find their way into the multitudes to create a new understanding of the world and our place in it. A plant that grows fallow and sends itself to seed only serves to enrich the soil and thereby renews itself. The human conversation."

"Seeds that go nowhere. So what happened?"

"It has…slept, gone dormant, but not gone. People out there don't even know evil as a concept. They have no great points of reference for knowing threats, and not knowing warning signs, they have no reason not to step to the altar and offer their necks."

Kenda accessed this reference and was sickened by the pairing. She saw the connection; lambs, fluffy creatures, lead off to be morged, butchered into pieces for consumption. She nodded for XY to continue.

XY continued, "A populace who actively casts a piece of themselves in with the machine, are easier to lull and be soothed by that machine. It does not seem separate from them. But is it evil? Distracting, annoying, maybe, but it may only be recognized as evil when we know what it turns our attention from. Benign evil, if you permit the paradox. People, always have had to choose how much invasion to allow. Is what you have witnessed truly benign? Or has the emotional buffering cushioned our sense of outrage?"

"Benign, harmless? Evil?" How do they work together? Let's see," Kenda focused and attempted to assimilate, but something-a connection distracted her, "a paradox is two ducks."

XY laughed. "Did RiEF teach you that pun? Delightful. Keep going."

"Okay, the real definition of a paradox sources as two seemingly opposite ideas that are true. How can there be a harmless evil? Either something is evil or it is harmless. It can't be both. Maybe it is also like king's coin? Taking the king's coin leads to being under the king's control? That kind of relationship could be harmful, but it would seem good because of the credits that the king is offering."

"Yes." XY replied. "The word I mentioned earlier, metaphor. Metaphors depend on creation, creating a third concept-a connection, which gives rise to concept, up from the murky waters of the unknown, pulled forth from the prehistoric mists. Communication is how we make sense of the world around us-our reality. This conceptual tool makes unto the world something newborn of the interconnections-the co-mingling of the attributes of two things. When discoursing on a topic, and our words are not enough, our phrases and sentences, paragraphs fall flat. We tend toward metaphor to strengthen understanding."

"If we speak about something and the listener cannot understand the enormity of a problem, we can make understanding with words in a new way through metaphor as with using the words caust and holo and we'd arrive at all-consuming fire, the fire that took everything."

Kenda accessed this holocaust word and she shut the imagery down after a minute. She shivered and said, "All consuming fire. That doesn't seem to explain it all, but I see how that would foster understanding. To approach the truth."

XY continued, "True. Pairers have difficulty in producing the metaphoric. That loss has locked us in platitudes of routine that don't shake a tree of knowledge, but rather build up an iron curtain, and spew forth script. Days go by as any other and none know to be enraged. How we spend our days, is how we spend our lives. So, how did you spend your days?"

"I spent them charging and sending, pushing product and sending. But pairing is a slight shadow of metaphor, isn't it?"

"It makes light of metaphor almost. It is functional because there is only one purpose to it-to incite a fervor for a purchase of product- and there is nothing it gives to the world if no third and greater sum is created. Consumption is not creation. They do not seek to further knowledge or understanding. You are different because your pairings suggest a leaning towards creation."

XY saw the effect that her words were having, but they were still missing their mark, so she asked, "What were your days like, before Spine? I've listened to and harmonized with some of the memories you have archived so far, and they are heartbreaking. Are there others that had meaning for you, but you had no words to understand them? Just tell me anything you remember about your life before sourcing."

Kenda thought back again to her days before becoming Spine. Nothing mattered in that time, except for charging and sending and spreading product. But, she did try to do things like talking to Dayzee and talking to Jernull. She reflected on those times and surprised herself by realizing that those were the only times that she remembered feeling anything. She shuddered, sipped her brew and closed her eyes to think. "I remember so little. I was only vaguely aware time was passing at all."

"We used to play a game called TopPart, which was a name that had been changed from its original name, the original name being, Together Apart. It was all over the network for two weeks. Users sat in a circle to boost their broadcast power. Some would close their eyes. The game consisted of tapping at a Ceramicat chasing its own tail around in a circle."

"We have data on that game." XY interjected. "The average user viewed 14,400 ads on the back of the cat."

"I felt sick when I was playing, you know, dizzy? I felt like I was going to throw up, and then I-I collapsed, where we sat. I felt myself losing consciousness. I reached out. I asked for help. I passed out. I don't know for how long. When I awoke, I couldn't see well. My vision was blurred. As things began coming into focus, I saw the same ring of people tapping away. No one had moved. No one spoke to me or came to find out. My head was throbbing. I rolled over, and I tried to get up. I begged someone to help me. I EEMed the people around me; no one responded. I dragged myself up to standing. After the daze wore off, I ate something-about 10 ThinBananas, and I began to feel a little better. There was a counterpiece app that registered my intake of ThinBananas, and it messaged me-*Congratulations, you have not had a ThinBanana for two days!* I realized that I had spent two days playing that game without eating!"

Kenda tried to source other words to describe the situation to XY. She sourced the word addiction.

"That is an appropriate word because addiction makes a user exclude most every other aspect of life to favor the addiction."

Kenda nodded, "I see what you are saying. Towards the end, I remember feeling so disgusted by the trash that was on the ground and everywhere, but the trash was also in my mind."

XY paused to make sure the recording equipment was still capturing the stories for the archives. "THAT is a good metaphor. Do you see the meaning you created with that?"

"Yes. Trash as words, as thought, as state of mind."

"Excellent-and if words make our meaning, then-?"

"Then trash words make trash talk make trash thought make trash actions to trash world."

"That is an accurate depiction of transactions that go on all the time. What else do you remember?"

"I remember sitting at a DrinkCoffee! House, chatting, vidding and EEMing with my friends. Dayzee began showing us a vid. We all tilted our heads together for faster uploads. We all sat there swapping vids of bangers and falls and aggressive marketing campaigns where people got stepped on. We just kept saying, 'Oh, watch this one...look at this guy get his lotion pot smeared back on him...here is the one where two Freshies walk right into each other and keep slapping off credits...watch this vid of a boy who was mauled by the VirtuOso bear...Oh God, he vomited...' It went on like that for hours. Then, when we leaned our heads back, our necks were sore."

We drank more DrinkCoffee!! Then the conversation turned to earning credits. Someone started, but I don't remember whom.

"I just heard that eating thin bananas helps with horxmone levels!"

"No way."

"I heard from someone that this girl got 3500 credits just for sending 200 Coolwalk EEMs a day for a month."

"That is true, I think I heard something about that."

"I read on the parshals that blue Funlight is good for your skin."

"D'uh. Everyone knows that. But did you know that SOLARFLAIR! Funlight activates muscle centers to help with Coolwalking!?- and that red Funlight helps brain thinking."

"No! I got to get me some red Funlight before the big celeb test if it helps brain remembering!"

Everyone laughed, but I didn't feel like it. The others tapped the P_ear consoles to accept the SOLARFLAIR advertisement and the credits flashed in our minds, '*Thank you for creating a genuine friendly conversation about SOLARFLAIR brandproducts.*' I declined the credit and set my console to quiet mode. I had an urge to go find Jernull. I dropped the Thin Banana on my tray was about to EEM about how great it was, but for some reason- I didn't. I got up and walked away-and I don't think my friends even noticed or cared."

As the memory faded, Kenda put her head down on the table. Using the new words she had assimilated from her DNA, she now both-knew the word ashamed-and felt it. But there was also a powerful sense of pride that washed over her because she could now both understand and express how she felt.

She picked her head up, "XY, you know how SympaticoCouch feels with you, well, when I got home it seemed broken that day, it couldn't read me right and kept crossing emotions together, first purring, then sighing, then humming. I don't know."

"It seemed confused?"

"That might be it. Yes, that word seems to fit. But why?"

XY smiled. "I think you are in love-with ideas-and someone who loves ideas as much as you do. The couch was trying to process complexity, and it isn't programmed for that." XY paused to let Kenda work this out. She had helped others before, and she knew how hard emotional knowledge is to source. When understanding seemed to dawn on Kenda's face,

XY continued, "Love and hope are the single most important themes that ever were."

"What is a theem?" Kenda assimilated the word from her DNA archives. "Oh, the main idea of the writing. Love. She walks in beauty like the night. Hope. Hope is the thing with feathers that perches in the soul."

XY nodded appreciably, "Nice connections. Your archive is working perfectly. You certainly got more out of your Info Pairing degree than they ever dreamed you would. There is a saying-a mind stretched-stays that way."

Kenda felt the words come at her with all their complexity. The ideas splashed inside her head, disturbing the waters of thought. From this ebbing tide came a small, cresting wave that poured over the cracked, dry earth of her desert mind.

❧About Another Room

When they had finished recording, XY brought Kenda to a room, "Behind this doorway, is what we call the 'Room within a Room'. I'll be back later to get you. There is food and water inside and a place to rest, but nothing more. That is precisely the point." XY let Kenda inside and closed the door without locking it.

Kenda sat down and waited for hours and heard nothing. She nibbled some food and it was delicious; she drank, and the water tasted clean and cold. She heard the snap of her food and the spill of the water into the glass. Then, more nothing. No sound from anywhere. She ran her hand along the walls and heard nothing. She marveled that this cavernous room held such a great deal of silence. It began to bother Kenda, who had never heard so much silence before, even in the Sanctuary stackrooms, there was chatter and murmurs and shuffling organic payprs. But, she got used to the quiet and felt her mind and self-go quiet. It was then, with her mind unclouded, that she began to think. She thought randomly, slowly at first, but then more feverishly in all directions and on every subject, her mind running and wandering alternately.

That is exactly how XY found her when she returned to check on her. She noticed Kenda's slackened posture and hands folded in themselves. She was the picture of composure and ease. XY offered, "Now that you have found silence, access song or art, or better yet, both."

Kenda looked up at XY who quickly retreated and closed the door again. Kenda closed her eyes and accessed Source from within her- "song." All of a sudden the room within the room erupted in sound. Kenda's eyes snapped open and her heart beat so fast, she thought she might pass out. She re-focused and listened and a wry smile spread from ear to ear. Kenda leaned back and soaked it in, every fiber of her, a living chord, resonating notes from within that room within a room.

There was a wall of sound and it boomed and moved, coming in like jagged lines and smooth elliptical, sine waves rode over and back, rolling hops of silken chimes blended with voices, melting into wordless undulations.

Kenda added the other search-"art". Colors lit up her mind in broad strokes with bright stars, amber waves, ochre faces, midnight hues dancing in circles, and yellow lines slanting sideways became green tangent lines that melted into clocks and a half-smiling woman, dappled Sunday afternoons...spots, slashes, splotches, bold minimal primary-colored impressions with black foundations and tangerine on terra cotta roofed houses with turquoise verticals.

All the music and colors and forms weaved, danced and spun through her mind. Kenda thought, "I have found the room. The most limitless room in the universe was-is right here with me-all the time. Why did I never use it before?"

The following day Kenda found herself wanting to record more for the Archives. Kenda had felt guilty about her self-discovery because she worried about Jernull and Dayzee. XY and RiEF had been searching for them, but without much success. It helped her to keep their memories alive. She went down to record another one that came back to her. It was about a conversation with Dayzee and others sitting and talking around a café table.

She remembered that she was the one who started the conversation, "I think my Winraise is broken."

Dayzee sipped her Shugso. "Shugso, the soda of cool POPularity! They really know what they are talking about. This stuff is great, I mean, it does pop in your mouth, and it is popular, and it has surgary in it. People should drink it all the time!" Dayzee tapped acknowledgement of the credit boost.

Kenda said nothing to this. Clearly, Dayzee was trying to cap some credits to pay her apartment rent. She tried again, "I think my Winraise is broken. I have to raise it up and push it down myself. Isn't that interesting?"

Her friend Ulik replied, "I just heard that at the Miss INFO Pageant, *Coolwalk!* is planning to enhance the user experience by shuttle-pushing event goers; we won't even have to walk anymore, the ramp will shove you along. It's going to walk for you!" Ulik slapped off credits.

Dayzee replied, "*Coolwalk!* in cooperation with the Lighthouse brand PanyKirki Fairgrounds will make a fun and new and improved event, gar-n-teed. It will be light and easy, breezy-breezy."

Kenda turned to Dayzee, who was normally was a good info pairer, and said, "Dayzee, that didn't make sense. The Lighthouse always has an independent sponsor; they don't pair with credit sending companies. They save their info pairing for the pageant day."

Dayzee turned to Kenda with a curious expression and nodded her head with a slight twitch.

The memory faded. She shuddered at the memory, and shut off the recorder. As the unease settled in, she did not even need to source the word sorrow; she knew it because she felt it.

XY came into the recording room. "We have a minding mission this week. I won't be available for your training much over the next few days."

Kenda asked, "I want to go with you on it. I need to look for Dayzee and Jernull. I can't just keep doing this. I need to act. I feel like that would help me and maybe help them."

"We are searching for them. Dayzee is hard to pin down because her EEMs float. Typical of her—condition. We have been allocating resources to it. She hasn't been home for a while. Jernull doesn't register as well because of his unique P_ear unit. We will find them though. And of course, we'll help you if we can. I can train you, as I get ready for this next one."

"That would mean so much to me."

"I know. I am sorry about this. It must be difficult not to know where they are."

"It is. Thank you for all your help."

"Hope and love, remember?"

Kenda smiled. "Yes, the magical themes. So, is that the reason you come down here?"

"One of them, but RiEF also left me a note that you had a query that the archives weren't clear on."

"Oh, yes. I can't yet understand the Source information on the newer history about how the pairing of emotions and furniture came about."

XY came over to the recording station and adjusted the five silver bracelets on her forearm. She drew her legs up sideways into the chair and settled into the cushion before she began.

"SympaticoCouch was a division the company that was formed when an ad agency and the world's largest fast food company merged. They made the emotional couch and paired it with the P_ear-so that advertisers could pair emotional responses into ads through people, to motivate people to favor their products.

"So, they wanted emotions in people to connect with the couch."

"Yes, but don't miss another interest, at first the emotional connection with people was set up to work the controls on the couch, true, but the real reason they designed the system was for the advertising side-to set up the emotional implant to make it easier to juice people to sell other things, too. Everyone wanted their furniture to feel with them, without realizing it meant other things to the company."

"Interest at play."

"Yes, king's coin, when we throw our lot in with a machine, we may not know all the things that we are giving up."

"So, what does the food production have to do with it?"

"Seeds are a remarkable delivery model, they contain source, they reproduce source, they are source. From them, springs the next generation. The final gesture before the death of a plant is to produce seeds, source for the following generation. They are free producers. There is no money in that. FlatVeg and ThinBananas leave behind only piles of wrappers, from which nothing comes. You can't reliably brand a plant, but a box can be copyrighted, and thereby owned."

Kenda fought back the urge to tap into a P_ear console that was no longer there. She also suppressed responding with the ThinBanana tagline. Old habits and training remnants of the person she was. Instead, she asked, "What about the other products?"

"What else is altered from its natural state?"

Kenda searched her mind. She shrugged.

"The sun used to shine and grow the seeds. Now filter panels alter sun rays into Funlight, and Funlight can't grow seeds, because of a spectral imperfection. Only sunlight in its true form, its source, can do that."

"How do you grow anything?"

"We found a way to access the sun from the wave filter panels-you saw it during your scar ceremony. Some of the grids are offline above our shelter here, and we rerouted the signal to indicate that they're fully functioning. We are stealing back our public domain."

Kenda sourced public domain. "Public domain sources as a work that has transferred from private ownership into the culture, and is no longer owned by an individual and is instead owned by all. Free access for all."

"Yes, it has to do with equalizing benefits to all members of a society toward creating a public good. There are ebbs and flows in sentiments in society and sometimes that means systems are breaking down. You may have noticed other system problems, yourself."

"I have. My Winraise wasn't working."

"Systems have a way of patterning like that, birth, growth, dis-integ-ration, death, rebirth and so on. Seeds are planted. They grow. They go fallow and are reclaimed into soil and thrown seeds remake the plant again."

"Mmmm. Where are we now in that cycle?"

"The end of dis-integ-ration. We think. You see the systems breaking down? When that happens, something is coming. Did you ever get data packets from The Bard of Sval?"

"Yes, they were corrupt. They didn't work right."

XY smiled a cat-like smile, "Sort of. Tell me what they did."

"They just pushed out the same words over and over again to the mindscreen, "Repetition is not enough. Repetition is not enough. Repetition is not enough. Repetition is not enough."

"Did they ever do anything else?"

"I got one, one time that finished a 40-count repetition with the words, "Creation prevents disintegration. Oh, gaw! That was Spine, yes?"

XY nodded, pleased with the deduction. "The Bard of Sval. Do you know why we started it? It is a lovely pun. QRoSe created it. A very long time ago, there was a place called

Svalbard. It housed a living source, they were seeds, actually, they were held in suspension, dormant, like our Source, but vital to humanity. Original, also like Source, tied to things, tethered to real change, real experience. There is so much they have in common, so we used it to make a data packet aimed at changing people's minds-giving them an alternative. It seemed a natural match to draw allies, and feed minds."

As she considered this, Kenda tucked her natch hair behind her ear, most of her nanophotons had faded. There was a ghostlike remnant of the coloring and bransponsor overlays throughout the strands, but without hair upgrades, the original color was reasserting a replication of its own.

Kenda looked up as she connected the metaphor and said, "Feed minds. Comparison of eating and reading, both nourish."

XY nodded and smiled. Then, she asked her, "Did you ever get sick after eating ThinBanana?"

"Yes, many times. Usually, it goes away if you eat a pink healthy option pouch."

"How many of those did you have to eat?"

"20 pink pouches for every Thinbanana, you've eaten."

"Do the pink pouches cost more in credits than a ThinBanana?"

"Yes, why?"

XY waited.

"Ohhh. I see. Profits."

🕏 Proliferation

Whenever Kenda ate meals with the other Spine, she always heard new ideas to turn over in her new consciousness, some new depth to wade.

On this morning, she came in during a long pause. Spine respected silence almost as much as they did language; they have always been that way. Each was reverently waiting on the speaker to begin. Finally, the speaker, a young girl standing at the far end of the table, whose calling number was 193.H462, spoke,

> "A pairing is just placement
> two words,
> simple basic
> -building with worn blocks.
>
> So metaphor, nexus of meaning creates-makes
> a third
> the meaning merged.
>
> But, winding like DNA
> Resisting tension
> Abolish, preserve, transcend
> Aufheben."

The table rang with tapping on metal drink cups, each acolyte nodding appreciably.

Kenda recited the words in her head and they sounded like an echo; something new, its hour come round at last, slouched its way toward her consciousness, wading in the deep to be born.

❧ Chapter of More Sourcing

"Accurate citation is important because it provides a connective record of..." {this record was partially deleted by the ABCC Dump Protocol}   *--Source: CHICA PAMLA Style Manual ~Final Printing~ (Exact Publication Date Unknown).*

Later that night, as they were working in the stackroom, replicating payprs to transcribe new additions to the Archives, RiEF told Kenda, "We do know approximately when the Digital Archive Project sources became compromised. It was after the advent of the Citation Referendum. This was a piece of legislation before the Senit that proposed that bibliographic citations could be optional, as they were cumbersome and not necessary, since all the information was digitized. The world barely noticed when it passed overwhelmingly."

Kenda sourced citations. "So, without citations, nothing was there to trace information to its source material? No linkages between information?"

XY nodded. "It made things difficult to sort and reference and made it impossible to verify research. At the time, due to the unique circumstances, the Spine would not dare speak out or weigh in, but they found followers through a cooperative final printing of the CHICA PAMLA style manual. It was a subversive guide to purists.

The digital library was fine, until the DAP protocol began exerting itself in an unpredictable way. This happened because funding for the massive maintenance and storage became unpopular with fiscally-minded voters. Advertisers were losing money and looked for financial assistance and the money saved by dumping works kept many a company from closing. But as for the continuity of information, the damage was done.

From what we can ascertain, when the protocol began to run off the rails, the result was small data lapses. But eventually, it began picking off whole entries and then, whole works. They remedied most of the issues in an effort to fix this, but the end result was that inaccuracies abounded. Nothing could be traced to Source materials. Works had become untethered from their originals. Some things remained because their access was so high, such as the popular antique GOLD AND BOLD recordings. Those things were immune from errors because they were what the public accessed in large numbers."

"Why couldn't they keep everything by paper pulp again or recover it?"

"They would have, but the explosion of the museum released a spore." RiEF paused and looked away. "It made paper impossible. Paper was grown, and harvested from the ground, and then made into strips." RiEF held up a stack of organic payprs that they were sorting for emphasis, "We created this grown papyr to substitute-to keep a record-a living record that you've read from in the reading rooms. We recreated it as closely as possible because paper was the most creative transmission system human kind ever imagined."

"You mean Source?" Kenda offered.

"Yes. They are one in the same."

"Tell me how the Spine became guardians of Source."

"When the forests of paper pulp were dwindling, the Consorcium helped to print what became known as the Spine Manual. The Spine made contact with private collectors who got the message sent in the pages of the Chica Pamla Style Manual. The Spine copied the private collection and preserved a second copy on DNA. That was the called the Second Gathering; the museum was known as the First Gathering, when people gave up paper and started digitizing."

"So, why couldn't they save everything if it was digital?"

"The Dump protocol had compromised the digital archives, remember, with the deletions that the lack of funding caused. Some things do bear saving, but who decides what is worth keeping and who pays are always the question to the public. The algorithm was given too much power but without any oversights or protections. Without guardians who have no interest or insurance working against them to protect the Source…"

"It will be at the will of the moment, or the will of those with interest. King's coin."

"Yes. Those who seek to own your hunger will keep you from making food."

"That is like the ThinBanana, no seeds means you have to keep buying, no public domain."

"Spine thought that the best defense at the time was to hide Source and themselves. It has become our biggest shame. We became seed keepers." She touched her scar. "Source is a great metaphor for seeds because they are both wonderfully effective carriers."

Kenda considered this. *Plants grow from seeds. Plants give off seeds. Those seeds grow more plants. They create a sustaining cycle. Carriers-bringing something, creation.* "What *is* the true nature of Source?"

RiEF said, "There is a poem about this."

"The long watch of mountains, stars.
Source is what the dreamer sees.
A stretch across infinity-
A witness to totality.

A shelter to stinging storms.
A bank to everbreaking tides.
A raised fist at a scrambling beast.

The story, a survivor's struggle
to edge out of darkness.

It is the primal blazing firelight
The torch that first pushed back the edge of night.

For the lost and left behind, it is cosmic witness.
The words that sing, that salve, that save.
Smashing the frozen abyss-
And shielding our vulnerable forms
against the arctic wind of indifference--
The traveler's rest, the starveling's star."

Kenda stared at her. "…"

RiEF smiled and sighed, "Yes, that too. The wordless. The silence. That which is not yet named. Source breathes life. From the conceptual ashes of the mind, story is exhalation."

"Source is powerful."

"*It is* a creative force."

"But if that is Source, is that what Jernull is seeking? You told me once that you read his works."

RiEF tilted her head in deep thought. After a time she said, "He is interested in another type of carrier-not creation, but investigation. His interest is not in the ethereal questions, but the kind that reveal, that expose, that share, but with particular attention to precision. It fosters another type of understanding."

"When you find him, I mean, if we can find him on this next mission, I think I can help his cause with something that I sourced."

RiEF smiled and nodded. "The sharing. He would love that, I am sure. Spreading the seeds was our mandate. As to finding Jernull, we are looking, but he's tripped his feed." She stood and brushed her cloak smooth. In the meantime, it's time we broke for dinner!"

🐦 What Kenda Learned at Dinner about Organic Snap

Kenda ate dinner with QRoSe and the Spine acolytes that night. Sitting at the end of a long room on a cushion, she munched a long orange stick.

"This is delicious. What brand is this?" She said out loud. Her hand instinctively went to the side of her head to broadcast a food fave EEM. Again, reminded of how her P_ear was long gone. She blushed at her compulsion to EEM, looking around at those around her. Instead of being derisive, they all tried to respond at once to her queries, respectfully.

"They are carrots. Picked by hand."

"They have no brand."

"They have no jingle or tag line-they make their own sound."

"They come from the ground."

"They green and feed."

"Started as seeds…"

"just one, makes energy of sun."

"The light that's sold in Funlight now—"

"Was once ours."

Kenda smiled and thanked each of them, chatting quietly with a few about the process they called photosynthesis.

When she was done, QRoSe, who was sitting near her asked her, "XY mentioned that you might want to get more historical information about the grow rooms?"

Kenda said, "I never want to be blind again. Yes."

After they'd eaten, QRoSe, got up from the table and Kenda followed her. They wandered out of the room and down a hall with green glowing lights. Kenda chewed her last carrot purposefully. *It tasted like… It made the most wonderful snapping sound…* there was a depth to it that made her feel full.

QRoSe led her to the garden, explaining how their buildings were hidden under SolarFlair wave light generators, huge panels of stolen technology hacked to seem like everything was functioning normally, but enabled to reflect the sun into the gardens.

She pulled a leaf from a basil plant at her feet and handed it to Kenda, "Try one." Kenda took the leaf and eyed it, it was a deep green, curved and veiny. Kenda chewed it, gently; it had a mild, pleasant sensation.

"Wow."

"Beautiful, isn't it."

"Mmmmm...yes. It's all in the ground?"

"It all originates there, grows from there."

"A source of sorts?"

"Yes, RiEF shared the metaphor we use, right?" said QRoSe smiling, "all things flow from Source. She's big on metaphors, as am I. XY is big on metaphors too, but very small on helping out in the garden!" QRoSE smiled, pleased with her own wordplay. "Whatever. RiEF's a good reference, XY is out there digging for minds to sow, so she doesn't have time to mind the digging. Sorry, I love puns. I know they're bad."

Kenda couldn't help but smile. She'd never heard anyone so in love with making words work in different ways.

QRoSe said, "While we're headed down, access source for definitions of root cellar or cold storage." She took her along the plants and into a cold room in the ground, which they reached by a narrow staircase made of broken plasmold mesh that wound around a giant center pole.

Kenda searched her mind and the information assimilated into her consciousness. "Root cellar. A place to keep something. They are cool and dark. Specific temperature ranges are key. Prevents spoilage...and saves them for future use."

QRoSe nodded, "Right. Good sourcing. Touch these." She lifted an enormous lid off of a containment unit.

Kenda peered in and saw a mound of wispy things. She reached in and took a handful. They were smooth and they slid easily through her fingers, back into the container. Kenda scooped another handful. She let them go again. One by one, and then several at once, gained traction and tumbled back into the container. They almost seemed alive. "Seeds. Such small things."

QRoSe nodded in agreement. Her multiple silver spiral earrings tinkled in unison. "But together, vast as the universe, renewing, the ultimate carriers, not perfect replication, but vehicles of exponential proliferation."

Kenda considered this with all the knowledge she'd gained since she'd come here, "They carry their own world unto themselves. It is a perfect metaphor for Source."

"Without Source, a mind goes to seed." QRoSe chuckled at her wordplay.

Kenda pushed for a pun to match QRoSe, and she found one, as she accessed Source on synonyms for treacherous ground, "Empty mind fields become…mine fields."

"Yes." QRoSe laughed softly, and then grew quiet, drawing in the full import of this comparison. Then her smile disappeared, "…hmmm…Empty minds *are* dangerous." Her voice was tinged with something hollow, ringing with a vast sorrow, like she was weeping for the whole world.

❧ Light on a Face

"Kenda," RiEF asked, at their next archive recording session, "Let's try to record a positive memory today. Can you remember something good?"

Kenda had to think very hard. "Radka, Dayzee and I sat around sending and resending. It was bright outside, the Funlights were in full HazeOrange. Radka's hair, gold and black and bronze with horizontal blue streaks denoting her brandsponsors, pulsed in a circular pattern. She laughed because she kept missing the shot in the game we were playing. Swiping and slapping on her P_ear, she tried desperately to get the dust to scatter correctly in the game. She couldn't do it. I think that I remember this clearly because there was such… beauty. Lights lit her hair, radiating out, she laughed with her eyes and her body shook with...happiness. Would the word mirth work, too?"

"Either would work, happiness is a state of delight at life, mirth is like that, unrestrained-joy."

"Joy without restraint, ecstasy, bliss. Yes. I like those too."

"What about the memory is beauty?"

"Radka with her hair and her laugh. Dayzee..."

"I know that will be hard to recall." RiEF put her hand on Kenda's shoulder.

"Dayzee is...was what passed for what I now sourc...I mean, I now *know* to be a best friend. She and I blundered through everything. It doesn't pair well with friend because even though there was closeness, closer than Radka even, whose death I never mourned, but it is as close as possible given our tendencies. I want to try to find her and Jernull. Bring them in, if we can?"

"That is the plan. XY and I are trying to set one up. I know it is hard. We have been trying to gather data on her movements for you, but her system is scattered. We can't get a good read.

Once we have a direction for the next minding mission, I will get you some Footmen boots; XY will have to train you how to use them. They are really heavy in the heel, but they are powerful, as you saw when XY took down two Footmen. Anyway, we know how much you want to share what you now know. Most acolytes try, with mixed results. I think you have given us good information for the Archives and I know you have some really amazing contributions ahead of you."

Kenda blushed. "I hope I can make some. I feel honored to be a part of Spine. I feel like I have a home here, and I want to give back if I can."

"You have definitely made an impact on XY. She's thrilled that you helped crack the DNA impediments with your perfect source assimilation. But now, let's try another route here for the archives. You pick anything at all that you remember."

"Dayzee always invited me to her product releases. I always came. She sent me EEMs all the time, sometimes asking how I was. I would EEM her...and..." she huffed a breath full of anger. "Farce. I can't...Why do people get Twitch- why! Why? I am so... I am so.. angry. I have no words.. mad.. incensed...furious..." the words poured from her, expression, unrestrained, "livid.. devastated...these things should not have happened! Radka-she no longer exists-Dayzee-soon-maybe, I don't know. The rage... the rage is a terrible thing. Outrage. The words are important. The words are important... accuracy.... accuracy. Dissemination, clarification ...knowledge...we need Source."

RiEF nodded, "It is true. They are mine fields, QRoSe told me about your connection of mine fields to empty minds as dangerous."

"The mine field for me is that I am too scared to recall some things. Because everything that I remember, in light of my new knowledge, makes me hate things I did, makes me hate the way things are. Not just the things that I see to be evil, but so much of the rest of it runs together, making most days as indistinguishable from the rest, the very *theft of life*. There wasn't a happiness, as I now understand what it means to be happy-it all seemed just a simple chain of events-going from thing to thing. That didn't feel like a life, it felt like a lie."

"I know. I am so sorry. We will do everything we can to help. We can be done for today if you need."

Kenda wiped her eyes and steadied herself and her resolve resumed, "I'm ok. This is important. This is important. I want the Archives to have Source material on the things I know. Let's keep going."

"Is there anything else you really want on the archive?"

Kenda stared through RiEF. She was lost in a search. She tried to recall another memory. Something important. There was one. The horror that had no name. She knew she had been avoiding recalling it. She did not like to touch on it, mentally; she did not want to bring it forward. "There is one that I need to remember. About a Push. It was sad, but sad isn't nearly enough to convey how it felt."

RiEF suggested, "Try to source deeper into the emotional descriptors to find a better word."

Kenda eased into the knowledge base. There were so many connections for sad, but her feeling drew her on to deeper levels. *Depressing. Yes, but still not precise to describe the whole of the situation. Wretched. Miserable. Terrible. Sorrow. Dreadful. Yes, also, but...? Tragic.* She sank her mind into the word. It seemed to fit on all sides.

"Tragic," She looked back at RiEF, "That's the right one."

"Only if you are sure you feel up to it."

Kenda nodded and wiped her face and eyes absently, trying to clear her head. She breathed out, signaling to RiEF. Her hands still shook, but her mouth was stone.

RiEF switched the referent for the file to PUSH encounter, unnamed PUSH/XY-KENDA INCARNATION. She looked up at Kenda, "I'm ready. Take your time. I've got all the tea in the world."

Kenda exhaled a laugh, and her sorrow was forgotten for a split moment. She gave RiEF a grateful glance and thought, *"The depth of understanding that these women have- that Source afforded- was nothing short of amazing."* Nothing made what she had to do easier, but it helped to know they understood her. It helped to know the right words. She inhaled once more and began.

"I had wandered off the CoolWalk into a new area. It was just another endless day re-sending EEMs, recharging my

console batteries and upgrading my hair color. I turned a corner
and bumped into a Push. And the Push grabbed my arm.

RiEF, you have to understand, I had never seen a Push move
unassisted before. I mean, they move sure, but only if pushed,
or being played with as a game, you know, in crowds. This was
also one of the first times I'd seen one alone.

He was taller than me. My eyes were level with his chin. I
got scared. I swear to gaw, I got so scared. I reacted. Like an
impulse. I shoved him. He tottered away, like always, but just
before he crashed into the wall, I saw him put out a hand to stop
himself. His eyes were still fixed. His mouth was still parted and
his expression, empty, but the arm. I went over to look in his
face. His eyes were half-open, and like all Pushies, he didn't
blink much. He was looking-focusing, somewhere behind me. I
looked back, but there was nothing there. When I looked back,
this Push, I swear, had opened his eyes full up, like in shock. His
mouth-a grin-this insane half snarling grin. I put a hand on his
cheek and pushed his face back into a smile. This made his eyes
droop. That was worse. And, then they flickered open again.
His left eye watered, began leaking. I brushed the drops from
his face. His smile began sliding, fading pulling down, until his
expression was just drawn and tight. It happened so slowly, that
I can't be sure it wasn't always that way. I tried to move him
toward the wall, turning his body and face away, but he wouldn't
budge. Most Pushies move, and I mean they move almost
effortlessly. This one seemed to refuse…like…what's the
word…stubborn, no…defiance, yes, he felt defiant. Of course, I
thought then that it was most likely my own wrong thinking. I
finally got him partially turned. I noticed that his eye was still
leaking. I didn't report him. I hated the idea that a bagger would
take someone who wasn't morged.

Then, I panicked. I just turned and started moving away. I
stopped and looked back, and it looked like he had his arm up.
He looked like he had his arm up. His face was contorted,
twisted partially toward me, you know, like he had turned it. He
felt a long way away from me, sealed in, walled off, but someone
forgot to close the last door. The last thing I see is the arm. Like
a warning, a wait, a please. Dear Gaw, I should have helped him,
but how? His arm was up. I swear- it was up-for me. A signal,

but I did nothing. He wasn't scary, he wasn't horrifying. He was in need...." Kenda finished in a small voice, "...and I did nothing. Tragedy."

Kenda put the backs of her palms to her eyes and eventually her whole arm covered her face, as her shoulders slumped onto the table. RiEF turned off the recording. There may have been more words, but Kenda could no longer utter them. She was still living their impact. There was more to say, but no will left to say it. RiEF carefully stored the recording strips and sat at Kenda's side, holding her shoulder, keeping the tea warm, in case. She tiptoed out when Kenda fell asleep.

❧ Accessing Source

After some time Kenda woke. Her face had pressed against the green plasmold recording table for so long that a long red mark punctuated the left side of her face. She wiped her face and looked around furtively, thinking at first that she had wakened from a diagnostic. When she ceased to have that wild animal look in her eyes, she went to look for RiEF, who was in the next room organizing pabrys into subject piles. She hugged Kenda and told her to go wash and collect herself. They arranged to meet later.

Kenda went back to her tiny room cutout. It was carved to resemble a cave. It was cold and dark and there was just a small table and bunk nook, where there was a stack of paypr books that contained parts of the Spine Archive. She grabbed another cloak and black pants set from the small shelf above the bed and went to change. When she came back, she lay on her bunk for a little while to process everything, *"There should be a reason. There should be something to gain from all this pain. This should all point to something. But, what if it doesn't? What if there is no meaning, or worse does all I have learned suggest a trashy, meaningless world? What if we are as inconsequential as seeds without a grow room? Every time that RiEF or QRoSe shows me source-one of the oldest ones-the bound paypr books-that feels real, I mean that feels like it has meaning. The words in the physical world-they tell stories, whisper from another time. Like my dream. I have no one to give my story to? No understanding. No listening. That sounds like morg. Like death. The death of Source itself.*

There is a great deal of emotional knowledge associated with death. Originate? Source. Beginning. All three pair well together. Dissolution was to end. Someone ending. That happens. People end. Lots of people end after they get the Push and Twitch. Radka ended. She had an end. People stop moving and morg. But not like Ceramicat, which doesn't morg, they shatter-not the same. Source and origin and beginning? To end, a person has to be moving and then stop, so a person must have an origin-a source? Do I know a source? Seeds. Seeds are a source-origin. Do people have source? I do not know my origin. I do not know where I began."

Kenda felt a new sensation, again, the pressure to know a thing. More than a casual query. Intense need. She accessed her Source knowledge from the DNA-coded Spine libraries embedded within her and fully engaged all of her mind to open them. She opened up her conscious mind and the information floods began. She assimilated whole categories, not just her XY series, but all of the Last Gathering washed over her, retreated and washed in again, her every sense alive with the tide.

She felt the legions of pilgrims that had come before her wondering this. *Where do I come from? The word, wonder. I wonder about my source.* She floated in the sea of her consciousness and began to swim toward the answers to origin. The answers were so close.

Kenda grazed the entire origin knowledge contained in the Archives of the Last Gathering. Horizons spun before her, points of light, lines, fonts, ports, vessel, chalice, well spring, roots…she smiled and felt the knowledge seas around her get wider, her inner space loomed infinite, and all around her waves upon waves began rolling in…*future and the past…from center, one builds, then entropy, decay/dis-integration that gives rise and integrates infinite… beginnings…and endings flowed as one until they became indistinct… there was no gap, no stop, only flow, source flows into dissolution…growing from ashes…dissolution into life…wave after wave…does destruction crave order or does order seek chaos? The only constant is dynamic-all are in motion, even in dissolution…?*

Kenda pulled forward out of her concentration and opened her eyes. She whispered out loud to no one, "Stored seeds preserve, but grow nothing. They end the cycle. The Spine *have* blackened the earth, *again*." She touched the scar under her eye and thought, *"This scar represents the vow to never be blind again-like RiEF frequently says, 'to mind something, one must be watchful.' The mandate was that we are not merely guardians, but gardeners.* As she went flying off her bunk, and down the passageway, she thought with delight, *QRoSe would love that pun.*

🍃 The Concept Rises

QRoSe did indeed love it. She found her cutting carrots in the kitchen, her considerable frame hunching over the small table. She shared the entire concept to her.

"Whoa. I can almost wrap my head around it." She washed her hands and sat down with Kenda at the tiny, plasmold table. "Almost." She kept muttering. "It rings true, but then what? What is the appropriate reaction to this philosophy? I'll speak with XY and some others, and get some other perspectives. Keep going in that direction. Follow that thought and see where it takes you."

"I will. I think it could be my real contribution, not just the Archives or the capricious result of my faulty grid."

"Don't you dare think that you didn't work through stuff on your own to get here. It was your thinking and pushing for answers that brought you to our attention. Just like you are doing now. Now, I've got to finish this dinner up. Go question everything and seek some more answers-research."

QRoSe rose to see Kenda to the door. Kenda helped herself shamelessly to a handful of carrots on her way out the door. QRoSe, even at her full height, with crossed arms, couldn't manage a convincing scolding glance at this thievery. Every Spine was aware of Kenda's carrot obsession.

❧ Thinking

Kenda spent a few days accessing every database, every paypr stack and talking to as many Spine as she could. She was a consummate researcher, which surprised no one. She queried all the experts, read all the payprs in existence, and churned over half a dozen ideas, connecting all these sources. Then, she went to the room within a room and thought. The silence was deafening, and just what she needed.

❧ Choice

When she wasn't researching, Kenda spent time wandering the halls of the Spine stronghold. She loved discovering what secrets these many rooms had to offer.

On one such foray, she came face to face with a door panel made of textured red iridescent plasglass. It was crisscrossed with a veined pattern that glowed from the light within the room. It had a certain pull about it; Kenda felt drawn to it.

She found RiEF down an adjoining passway and asked her to show her the room. RiEF unlocked it for her and said she would come back when Kenda finished exploring it. As a parting shot, RiEF motioned an off-you-go-but-don't–say-I-didn't-warn-you-way, "In there, you need to make good choices." Then she shut the door, and left Kenda to her exploration.

Inside, the room was comfortable and welcoming, cool blue and soft floors. It was a long, rectangular room, like a hallway. There was a little band of moving tread, like a CoolWalk!, which moved against her steps as soon as she stepped on it. It took some getting used to, but once she got the hang of it, she was able to walk and steady herself as the treadmill pushed against her gait. Because the tread underneath her moved, she never reached the end of it.

As soon as she reached a good pace on the treadmill, a vidscreen glowed to life on the wall in front of her and began showing images. It flashed images with each step she took, like a rolling viewfinder. At first, the images were blurred, but she found that if she kept her speed at a steady pace, they began to come into focus. She was seeing Spine rooms and common areas. The videos showed footage of RiEF in the stackrooms. She shouted for her, but RiEF kept working, oblivious. "Hmmm, no microphone," she huffed, working hard to keep walking so the vids kept flashing.

Kenda noticed something else, too. There were bolts on the sidewall that she could push. Out of boredom, she pushed a few. Doing so, changed what vids came up, and it also changed what vantage points she saw things from.

The vids clicked on and off, in unison with her bolt pushing…ABie in the listening room, monitoring P_ear sends. Kenda could hear ABie speaking, "…seek feeds with Morg taglines…"

Another bolt. The vids changed. She saw crowds at the Meeting Place, staring at the sky, waiting for the mid-day Funlight change. "-it's gonna be hueliscious in shades of burgunredash of green, cuz I order the whole Wintercoat color line from Funlights!!…"

"You know, I ordered the Orange Pico Pango, it's like mangorically orange, and by the way, don't look directly at it when the burning starts…"

The screen flicked to a vid of The Dollar Llama. "Glitterati-sparkle and shine,

You'll have a good time---"

Kenda ran harder. This seemed to help get rid of Dollar, but something new was coming. She could sense it. She couldn't look away. She watched a few more and fell into a pattern-a dull, plodding, rhythm, vids streaming with strident regularity. Her eyes did not blink with the same persistence, her lips parted slightly. She walked on. The mill kept spinning beneath her feet. She kept pressing new bolts in new combinations. She was having trouble remembering something that RiEF said; the vids drowned it out of her, "-*Oh that vid was nix! …That Funlight was huelicious…Oh my gaw, that was hilarious…This room has a physical noise in it. I feel tired-rundown…*"

Every time she pressed a bolt, it was followed by another vid on the screen. She pressed and pressed all day. She did not eat, and she did not notice the time. She stared, poking and watching, the furious clicking noise filled the room and she gave over her entire focus to the clicking and the images streaming out before her. It wasn't until she saw a vid of someone running in the path of a transport. From the remoteness of the small room, she felt paralyzed, but she kept running and watching. She shouted, "Stop! Please!" and shut her eyes against seeing the impact.

The transport made contact with the man and he slipped under the transport.

She ran up and tried to press her face against the shining screen, straining to see the fate of the man. Her legs flew behind her, stomp running to keep from being thrown off. She pressed the same bolt combination to try to restart the vid, "What happened? Was he okay? Did he morg?" Still nothing. She took her fingers off the buttons and stared at the glass. There was nothing there. She felt herself slow to a halt and slipped off the edge of the mill onto a floor. She felt the room warble and spin.

She said firmly, "I don't want to do this anymore!"

Kenda felt as if she were floating. She hit the floor and found herself lying in the smooth hallway on the other side of the glass door.

"Nicely done." This was one of RiEF's wonderful-make-you-feel-good compliments. Kenda may have appreciated it more, had she not been so loopy.

RiEF extended her hand to Kenda. "Let me help you stand up. 22 hours is a long time to be in the Platitudes." Kenda gave RiEF a questioning look.

"We set up that room to help new recruits understand their past. It is designed to work until the participant doesn't want it to work anymore. For some reason that is the best way to gauge the exact moment someone frees themselves."

"What an unspeakable pull that thing has. I did not think I was in there that long."

"That is the problem. A platonic seduction. We call it The rush without the fuss. It gives us vantage points that we believe in so badly, that they almost become real."

Kenda drew in a sharp breath of recognition, "That's what Push must be-when the walls become greater than the world."

❧Weeding

The grow room was the crown jewel in the Spine stronghold. Green spiraled everywhere. It wound around every upright surface. Flowers dotted the rows upon rows of fluttering leaves and stems. Pale, streaming yellow light cut through green angles and lit up veined fronds. Water glistened from everything scattering the natural light and making the room glow with faint reflected wisps.

On this day, QRoSe and Kenda worked together over the rows of hydroponically-hunched over the suspended root systems at their knees. They were weeding out the dead stock and feeding and pruning the new vegetation. Half the battle, QRoSe explained, was knowing where and what to cut.

"We must be careful because even though there is much that grows that isn't worth keeping, you never know what will be important later."

Kenda surveyed the plants around her and nodded. "Why not just keep all of it?"

QRoSe looked at Kenda with all seriousness, "There are some that clog the system, choke out those that need to survive, to live on and send out seeds-one day. There are some that spread and proliferate, like invasive species which take over and then the carrots would be lost forever, seeds are not to be spread irresponsibly and not irresponsibly left to seed whatever they claim. Ever vigilant needs be the gardener or her fields will be full of nothing fit to eat."

❧ Pruning

After leaving the grow room, Kenda jogged down to meet RiEF in the stackroom to get more information on the stories of the decline, just before the Last Gathering. One of the recordings was something called a telephonic message…

"Thank you for calling the Fairfacs County Library…. You have reached our after-hours line. This message is to alert patrons that we will be changing our hours as a result of countywide budget reductions. The new hours will take effect at branches in the area on midnight, July 4th. The Access Services branch, which is located at the Fairfacs County Government Center, will maintain its current hours for the foreseeable future.

Here are the new hours:

Regional Branches

Monday 1 p.m. - 4 p.m.

Tuesday 11 p.m. - 1 a.m.

Wednesday 1 p.m. – 3:30 p.m.

Thursday Closed

Friday Closed

Saturday hours remain 10 a.m. - 1 p.m. Odd weeks only

Sunday hours remain 1 p.m. - 3 p.m., even weeks only.

Smaller community branches will be closed until further notice. All renovation slated to begin this year will be postponed indefinitely.

Library fines will be increased 50% over last year's projections. If you have reference materials out over the 3 day time allotted, your fines will triple. Please see the DAP website for coming changes, as they have now assumed controls of all online catalogs nationwide. Thank you for your continued patronage of Fairfacs County Public Library. Good night, and good luck in your searches--BEEEEEP—

Kenda looked up at RiEF, "I sourced the words community centers, and it says that they are places of gathering for meetings, events. The branches are cut though? Plants, branches? I don't understand. Pruning like in gardening, cutting back, cut backs?"

"Financial cutbacks. They diverted money from these centers. The branches were smaller centers where they stored Source. The metaphoric name, branches, came from the appendages of an ancient plant called a tree that was destroyed by the spore that we released after the Cataclysm. A tree had branches that gathered sun light to feed the whole." RiEF gave her another audioCast to listen to. It sounded in her ear, cracking and snapping,

"The Public Dominion Quorum, in honor of the opening of the first Digital Archive Project Vidroom on the bulldozed site of the old NYPL, proudly presents a hardcopy of the newly printed CHICA PAMLA ~A Collective Style Manual. This will be its final printing as a commemorative edition. This will be a manual to be treasured and kept in private bookrooms everywhere. Order now and we will include the free supplemental Spine Manual insert at no extra cost. Order now, as this will be the last paper book in production, EVER! Available for a limited time. Order yours today. Imagine, the wealth of the proper sourcing laid out in one exciting edition!"

RiEF beamed, "It was the Spine Manual insert that led people with private collections of Source to have their books of bound paper retrieved, preserved, and protected by Spine. The manual was a warning that collections weren't safe against the deadly arboreal spore unless they were organically sealed. The Spine visited each collector and sealed their works and then kept an organic copy. The Ghdess is all that remains of the organic copies. She has for centuries taught us the same messages, but recently, she has uttered something new for us! Tomorrow, I'll introduce you."

🍃 Meeting with the Ghdess

The next day, Kenda was at work classifying and sorting seeds in the cold storage room. She was working on the fifth column of seed containers, when she came across scratches in its surface, where some clever Spine had written on. It said,

-.4° Fahrenheit
-The Bard of Sval

She sourced -.4° and found to be an optimal temperature for seed storage. But there was another entry under literature and a man called Bradbury who wrote a book with a very similar name. She was not able to source the Bard of Sval, but she did find a Bard of Avon who was a writer and a place called Svalbard, which she had already learned, was a Spine data packet, and a location that harbored a seed storage facility. Kenda thought, *"QRoSe must have made this sign, there were so many connections and word play."*

XY approached her through the rows and columns, and leaned over the container, "Kenda, RiEF told me that the Ghdess is ready to meet you now. Head over to the Haligen Hallway. Finish up here, and I'll meet you there."

Kenda smiled and nodded, "I'm so excited! More research!" She folded the last of the seeds she had sorted into the bin and tied her brown hair behind her with a knotted cloth. Then she shunted the remained seeds to their bins. When she returned the cart to the storage shed, she sprinted back down the rows and out into the passageways.

She met XY at the edge of the Haligen Hall, named for its glowing lights strewn along the waist level railings. Kenda thought of a pun on enlightenment that she made a mental note to share with QRoSe later.

They made their way down a ramp to a grey landing which overlooked a small darkened room. On the ceiling and the walls, everywhere, there were crisscrossing orange, tangential lines crossed by yellow half circles. The resulting patterns pulsed with a faint, intermittent light. The room seemed to shift at random. This made it hard to see her at first. Kenda even doubted she saw her.

XY smoothed her hand on an exposed side wall panel and a glow emanated from a corner of the room and began tracing throughout the wall until it revealed in stunning outline, the form of an old woman on the wall. All around her seemed to breathe yellow. Her amber eyes were lidless and her hunched form shook slightly. Kenda's eyes adjusted to the darkness. She moved forward and knelt before the woman.

She studied the Ghdess' eyes and shaking hands, but mostly her eyes, they were blank and wandering. Her visage scrambled again and reformed. She reached out a shriveled hand and grasped at something near Kenda's face and then her hand nestled back inside her yellow robe.

The woman seized a breath, like she was snatching it undeserved from the air. "I am recording, from this room of my own, because there is no more paypr----". The Ghdess coughed spastically before continuing, "...Everyone kept saying things are source, they were not source...form and meaning are carriers, but the shell... gives nothing in return...dead things that cannot bear...proliferation, seedless singles, bear nothing... They tried to hide my trove in an arc-to protect it, but they--". A blaze of dull light passed quickly between two electrodes on the wall and then faded.

The Ghdess did not notice. She pinched together an ancient hand, her holographic image bidding a Spine Shelving greeting from across the centuries and whispered, "Best laid plans-ove my sand men. Hour farther ooh ardent have in, hello bee thigh nay um, thigh king done come, thigh well bee dun honor'th says sit tis in have in."

XY whispered, "She still occasionally makes many mistakes because some of the DM protocol uploaded, too. For many years, she has said similar things, but since the latest replication was entered into Spine Source, she spoke new, something not of the programming and it began a new debate within the Spine. Your theories! It aggrieved us terribly, given our part in the Last Gathering. We are not sure about what to make of it. I'll show you." She smoothed the wall again, and this time it lit a green hologram projection of the Ghdess.

The image steadied and the Ghdess smiled, her image did not waver. She recited calmly, "Cultivation *is* the gathering. It is pure and raw harvest. Reap what you sow, but sow not, and leave your black scar on the earth. Gathering is but the half. If all things flow from Source, the gathering is but the half...only seed is the nexus-the sign of life and death..."

The Ghdess faded. Her light melded back into the optics embedded on the earthen wall and began racing around in a smooch on the wall until she was no more, reabsorbed awaiting recall from the organic data strands that looked like root systems from some angular ancient tree. The woman was again fully subsumed in the wall.

XY knelt beside Kenda, "This new information was never in her original messages. How it was that she came to produce it, we do not know. It was filed under calling numbers for philosophy and literature, but not agriculture. The Spine are at some type of crossroads now, with the discovery of you and your faulty grid, your lovely, holy, faulty grid." XY continued, "It is that fault that allows grace, it affords that hearts and minds coordinate, they do not grow in isolation. Now we know how to break through to many more people."

Kenda looked up at XY, as a pounding surf hit her understanding, something at last paired purely, she whispered, "One by which we feed, the other by which we continue. The other half, yes, or there will be no more gathering... dissemination!" Then another wave of understanding hit, "Two things in conflict-keeping, yet freely giving. Ownership is not what the world needs most."

"Can you connect that to any source?" XY asked, waiting patiently.

"Yes, the ultimate wealth of a society, its fertile grounds..."

XY nodded, "The access for all?"

Kenda pulled inward, sourced, thought and the connection finally burst through and spilled forward, connecting rivers to streams, oceans that fed all tributaries, unleashed and washing through her conscious mind, "Public Domain-that is the word, great sharing, for the world so loved the word...it must return to that, takes out interest and insurance, prepays for that knowledge to be available to all. How important that role was." Kenda paused. "Fairfacs, everywhere…the growing fields…The libraries, the branches. The physical places that were closed. The centers of community! Pillars…backbone…"

"…spine…"

👀 Jernull Takes the Lead

Jernull awoke with a thought-Kenda's public calendar. The last date on her calendar said she was supposed to be at Themall. He went to check.

He did not find her at her favorite Themall activity-the Maybewins outlet. He never made it that far. He nearly tripped over a morged body at the Footmen service center entrance. He found another one inside minus his trademarked steel-soled boots. He attempted a pairing as he stood between the two dead Footmen. Something paired here, larger than what is still here. A reason, an event that created this third outcome. Something plus the dissolution of the Footmen.

"Who did this? What led up to this? When did this occur? Where did they go? Why did this happen? How can I find out?"

There were two things pairing within him even now. The sense of wondering and the sense of revelation. *"Seeing, that's one, telling, that's two,"* he thought, *"and then an end product is the third thing, making of a third thing, the-what happened is the unit of transmission. Units can be sold-sold directly to the public."* That last part was not what thrilled him. What did thrill him was the transmission. *Mission. This is my mission-to make sure others know the answers. Something caused their .:Dissolution:. No, not the right word, not dissolution-their death.*

Sparks began to rise and flame within his mind. *"I could find out. I could. I know lots of controls in the P_ear unit's outer console."* He knelt down and tapped on the console, no response. *It can't be blown yet.* He tried to pry open the casing, but he had forgotten that all Footmen have a special lock on the interior. He made the appropriate taps and the grey console panel flipped up, with a whirr, into repair mode. He realized that all the time he'd worked with codes and P_ear systems he had never seen the inside of a Footman's console. He wanted to know what was in there.

He peered into maze of organic binders and lengths of grey strands…there lay an answer. There were all these dampeners, restricting flows and blocking responses while letting only specific strands freely transmit. The ones that were the strongest were the ones for predictability and pattern.

"Oh." he said out loud to himself, "Repetition... insurance against novelty."

❧ Bread & Circus

"This device will help you communicate emotionally with your furniture! When you laugh, your couch will laugh at you!"- P_Ear/SympaticoCouch launch tagline

Baitti Banburn, a large, pale man, was CEO of Bits and Bytes Inc. the massive global newsporting agency. He had made a fortune with the P_ear wrist console, and it allowed him to build the embedded version with a neural tissue grid for emotional transfer. Later, he went into Newsporting and developed the first Breviate and Parshal newsport formats designed to be cast and vidCast directly into the P_ear proprietary units. He also was personally and professionally involved with the Miss Info Contest, which honored Trending Newsporters.

Jernull's paternal figure invented Solarflair!'s Funlight Technology and sold it at an enormous profit to the Food Growers Association, so they could utilize it to block and only reflect certain spectrums of light and market them as Funlight! They hired a security contractor called Footmen Enterprises-*we do your legwork!* The company provided panel security against the Free Gardeners Coalition who attempted to steal sunlight to grow their own crops and keep their own unpatented seeds. Bits and Bytes put the Footmen in charge of P_ear unit maintenance and security, and from theft and tampering; their contract was written to cover the security of the units, not the user. P_ears were expensive to produce because of the added emotional amplification transfer grid of the SympaticoCouch! interface. For an additional fee, the Footmen also assisted in alerting the baggers, when units failed or users morged.

Even though his paternal figure was proud of his company and all he had built, Jernull made no secret that he wanted no part of the business.

It was just two weeks ago that the two men had sat, as all progeny-heirs do when it comes to agreeing on future plans, silently and uncomfortably. Baitti found himself head-on with someone he couldn't manipulate. Jernull found himself at a crossroads of conscience.

Baitti, this vast and vastly important man sat at the end of a wide, black, plastiform-glazed table. His immensity most sharply, was in his wide rounded chest, which was covered in armored plasmold plates. Thick, rolling arms draped across his chest. He had a steel blue tie and silver-tipped fingernails, that shone like razors. His hair, Bits and Bytes Blue, undulated between strands to show the logo moving from his temples around his head.

"Now listen, Nully," He leaned meaningfully across the table. A sideways grin smeared on his face. "This pageant is very important for the company. I am entrusting you to make sure it goes well. Just give the speech I EEMed to you."

Jernull who was looking down, rolled his eyes. Without looking up, he mumbled, "The speech? Yes, then, ok—well—I am Jernull of the Banburn, this month's MISS INFO Pageant's Honorary Field Marshal. This event is one of the most famous events, having the honor of recognizing the newsporter who has given the world the trendingist stories. In this case, it is Kitty Reed, the woman who wrote the Bits and Bytes series about crimeoffenders who disable walkway controls, causing joint pain and moderate discomfort to city joggers when transitioning over those points. Now I want to remind you all that—"

"I'm going to stop you there, Nully, I think you need to add in more product-focused bits. Why did you think we picked someone who wrote about CoolWalk!? Let me get you the list of sponsors again." He roared out to his assistant, Shilli, "Shilli! EEM Null that list of sponsors."

Shilli dashed in, hair ablaze in mangorical Orange and Bits and Bytes blue with just a slim part between the two. She nodded, and tapped viciously at her P_ear unit, and Jernull instantaneously got the list on his mindscreen. He immediately shook it away. Shilli resent it, and then she tottered back out to the outer office.

"Shilli! Keep putting the reminders on that list for Nully! Add the event to his Calendrix!"

Jernull cringed at his thunderous voice, bleaching out every other noise, "I have the list, paternal figure. I just wanted to get the full word out about the event, not just the Brandsponsors' names."

"Null, the only way to put on a production like this is to have major sponsors, and we don't want to let them down, do we?" Banburn's lips curled and froze on the last syllable. His teeth were jagged and their points headed in any direction they chose, creating a mountain range between his lips.

Jernull shrugged, but it looked more like a cringe than before. He did not care. He knew he couldn't win this battle. He kept thinking of Kenda and wondered why the Footmen were looking for her. His mind drifted as his paternal figure drilled, "...then you'll say on the Coolwalk! Looks good, feels soft!..."

Jernull's mind wandered. He had sent Kenda an EEM, which he generally didn't do, but he was just trying anything. He kept it simple so as not to arouse suspicion, "You missed your final." It returned a blocked signal. He did not know what to make of it.

His caution was well-warranted, because he got a message today before this meeting. BANBURN INCOMING: *Jernull, who is this girl? I got word the Footmen want to help her. Let me know."*

Baitti snapped his fingers, bringing Jernull out of himself, "Null, are you paying attention? I said I never got an EEM back about that Harkonna311371 girl? She still hasn't turned up, eh? Well, don't worry about it. I am sure I would have heard if the Footmen found her. I'll let you know. Ok, now about the speech, let me have a stab at the full opener. Here's what I am thinking- Welcome to the MISSINFO Pageant-sponsored by Coolwalk! *We walk with you and not against you!* and ThinBanana-*the thin banana for thin people.* I am Jernull of the Banburn. As Honorary Field Marshal, I know what a job it was to get over here, without Coolwalk!, it would have been lots of hard walking coming over here on the surface areas, let me tell you! Wasn't it great of the Coolwalk! company to get us these new walkways? Let's give a nice resend out to those guys, huh? You know, this event is one of our most EEM-worthy events, having the honor of recognizing the newsporter who has sent the most newsports! She's great isn't she? Miss Kitty Reed, looks great in that umbrella bikini, too. I bet she eats ThinBananas, huh?"

"Jernull? Are you listening? You are going to be leading this company someday, and this is part of your preparation to show me you can do it!"

Jernull met his paternal-figure's eyes, "If I had this company, I would want a new model. One that pays the Newsporters directly. A system that rewards the work, not the sensation, not the advertisers."

"That model won't work! Nobody wanted to pay for what was free, nobody wanted to pay for something they can get anywhere. When it was free, it did not have any value. You have to add value into the system or you have to sponsor-support it."

"Because the newsporters are the ones who are reporting the stories. Advertisers corrupt the system! It puts an interest in play!"

"There would be no newsproducts without it. Look, you'd need constant support to produce and even then, the end product may not be saleable. It has to be paid for in advance. End users wouldn't do that, especially when other people were giving it away for free. Users EEM from everywhere; everyone is a potential newsporter."

"The model could be simple, producer to end user. No interest, no insurance. Longer stories, more information. There are things going on that people should know."

"What things?" Banburn leaned in. Jernull shrugged, "There are other things going on in the world than things connected to brand."

"Things like Spine? Do you think they've taken your Harkonna311371?"

Jernull assessed his father's face. He did fear them. There was an interest here. "I haven't a clue. I just know that there are things that go unreported because it is unfavorable."

"No one wants to hear really unpleasant news. They want their news to be fun. It's just a bad model, Null. It will never work. People have done without newstories for so long. Newsports are more interesting and it gets credits for users.

Plus, they are short! And, you can never take interest out of newsporting. It is always there. Like I said, every user is an individual broadcast station. That is the role of the Footmen-to keep our system working. To complete the circle. A story without an advertisement is worthless because everyone can access it free and it lacks prior funding. Like ThinBananas, small stories are cheap to produce, easy to consume and can win the requisite advertisement dollars because we sell lots of them. If you mass produce small bites of a story and it gets viewed millions of times and that brings in money to keep the cycle going. Longer stories take way more money and no one finishes them. The public hasn't got the tension span."

Banburn grinned again. To Jernull, it felt like being stabbed.

Jernull demanded, "People could evolve to appreciate getting good information, real information?"

"People want vidCasts and newsports about fun things, safe things and foodstuffs. They don't want to hear things that scare them. They don't want news to take too long. They want free."

"Some things are worth learning even if it is hard, sometimes especially if it is."

"They need what we tell them to need. If you feed them, and vid them, they happily consign everything else to you. I think I know what methods work, Nully, I mean, look around." For effect, Banburn waved his arm around the glistening room. They were sitting in the top level of his high Crete tower, the very mink of fortune oozing from everything in the room.

Jernull sought his own mind for connections; he filtered and ventured into the mindscreen, accessed files. "There are some things that might need to be free. There should not be a price on things we need to know. It creates an imbalance."

Jernull turned his head away from his paternal figure's gaze and in the silence that followed, his eyes fell upon the shark on the wall, shellacked in a final, attack pose. It was a relic from the last viable era of the ocean before the remaining acres were sold to the FlatFish Aquafarming Company. Its glorious, shining mountain range smile and dead, glazed eyes caused Jernull to slump in his chair. It was a smile he knew well. He relented or rather, he stood up, "Just have Shilli EEM me the speech that you want me to give. I'll do it."

"That's more like it. You see, you can't take that tangential philosophy major too seriously. See Shilli on the way out, she got you a graduation gift from me. I've got some things to check in on. I'll EEM you later."

Jernull left and didn't bother to pick up his gift, so Shilli sent him an EEMinder that hit his P_ear before he left the building and he deleted it before he was home. He went by Kenda's door, but there were so many Footmen milling around that he went back to his apart-ment 3 builds over.

What could they want from her? Why was he getting blanks from his P_ear from her? A blocked EEM response like this usually meant that the user was dead. He did not want to entertain that. He couldn't find any Bagger alerts for her, so that was promising. He slumped into his SympaticoCouch! and cried, and the couch cried softly with him. Shilli EEMed the speech to his urgent inbox and it had 3 overlaid reminders that he had to disable individually. They would keep reminding him until he submitted a vidstream of him practicing the speech, which he did the next morning to get them to turn off.

XY was thrilled. She and Kenda stared at each other. They had talked many times about the lighthouse plan, and this was the thing that would put it over on the vote.

XY spoke first, "This makes so much sense. It means that the dispersal is right. The lighthouse is right. You gave me the insight on how we can convince the others. The scar cannot be our only mandate. Seeds must be sown, right? What we need now is a new beginning, since dissolution is at hand. Source should be planted. I will call a circle and see if they will agree to the lighthouse plan. You have to be there to back me, if I need you. They trust you."

"I would be honored. I also have one more thing-a request."

"Queries you never seem to run short of."

"This is different. I thought of something that I'd like to send to Jernull that could help him with his theories. He has a little knowledge and a little knowledge can lead him down the wrong path."

"Let's have RiEF source it for you. You can come on the Minding mission today. We are going to search for Jernull, Dayzee and a new prospect."

Kenda's face lit up. She was elated, and a wry, but triumphant smile spread slowly across her face, "I know just what to send him."

"Go see RiEF or ABie for a copy of whatever you are planning, and she can send it out with the forward scout team. Afterwards, come back later for boot training."

"You mean you're going to let me wear the boots on a minding?"

"Yes, if you don't mind."

"Gaw, even QRoSe wouldn't have allowed that pun. I'll be back." Kenda hustled out to find RiEF.

When Kenda retuned, XY was in her minding gear, hairstrands ablaze in yellow and a false P_ear attached. She also had on the Footmen boots. She had painted them to blend in with a sender's style shoe. She held out a similar pair to Kenda, who put them on."

"I have called a Spine Circle tonight. We need to be back for that. I think they are ripe to move on the plan. I already started polling members. Let's start your training. Here is your disguise that ABie made for you." She handed it over to Kenda. "Did RiEF send out the copied folio that you wanted to send Jernull with the scout team?"

"She did. And, yes, she made a copy first. You know she'd never let an original piece of Source out of her sight."

"Of course, that's reference people for you. Put the Sender disguise on with this hair overlay, and then switch the boots on, down there, by the top strap."

Kenda fumbled into her disguise. She attached the hairstrand generators, applied the fake P_ear, and pulled and zipped the rest of the purple sender clothes on. The hairstrands blinked to life, low-level advertiser colors, teal, grey and purple hairstrands that blinked for an obscure vertiser even Kenda didn't know.

"I feel weird." She brought her hand up to touch the P_ear unit. She brushed it with her fingertips in familiar patterns. For a moment, she thought she felt her mindscreen flicker, but it was just her imagination. She shuddered, remembering the tower of bodies.

"I feel the same, but, look sharp, there's no time. First, lift your legs up and down alternately, you know, march around."

Kenda tried to lift them, but they were frozen to the ground, "They're too heavy."

XY tossed her a control key. There was dried blood on it, which Kenda was pretty sure belonged to XY. "Slip it in your pocket. They won't work too far away from them." Kenda did as she was told. Now, she easily marched around the room.

"Good. Kick."

"Kick what?"

"This-" XY rolled a 400-pound plasmold seed container at Kenda, sending it barreling straight at her. Just before it ran her over, she kicked her right foot and it smashed the thing to splinters.

Kenda stared at it, wide-eyed in horror and muttered, "Effortless."

XY nodded, "like too many other things. The rush without the fuss. Training's over. Let's roll. Stop picking up those barrel pieces. We've got to go."

🐦 Light and Enlightenment

"Who needs the sun? Funlight is fun!" -Initial Funlight Tagline

"SympaticoCouch! Your feelings are our bottom line!"-Original SympaticoCouch tagline

The Lighthouse was a sign of nostalgia gone mad. Sometimes, a developer gets it in their head to build something old. They find big sponsors, in this case, Bits and Bytes paid to have it built, so they could resell the space for advertisers' events to be staged there. Lighthouses were remembered because so many small plasmold statues of them survived. This was similar to the reasons that Candy Lane recordings survived, so many millions sold and accessed kept it alive through the DMP protocol that wiped out other files.

The small, plastic replicas of the lighthouses were sold by the millions in the tourist trades of bygone eras and they did not disintegrate. They persisted in the culture, despite their total disconnection to meaning and purpose.

So many concerts too place at the Pani Kirki fairgrounds, from Shugso's GOLD AND BOLD Candy Lane replays; Coolwalk!'s .005-mile marathons; and the MissInfo Pageants were all staged under the blind eye of this oversized lighthouse, which broadcast no light whatsoever.

From the top of the tower, instead of light, they used to release ceremonial birds as a grand finale of many of the pageants and events. The interior had been used for many years to load the birds in pens, using a series of ancient cranks and gears. The birds would rise in cages to the top level and be released to fly out over the crowds carrying little broadcast stations on their backs. These stations would beam advertisements to the crowd that went off like firecrackers in the mindscreens of the users. Unfortunately, sometimes birds would release other unpleasant packets of their own making to the crowds below. All of this was very expensive to maintain, the birds, the mechanisms, the bird feces cleanup equipment, such that, in the last few years, since renovations weren't routinely done, the birds were catching in and stunting the gears, bloody gore was sometimes shot out of the top and then onto the crowds instead of birds. Consequently, the lighthouse fell into disrepair, disuse, until finally and recently, Banburn sold it at auction to someone simply called Liv Lem. Bits and Bytes was happy to be rid of the financial burden, and happy that it still served as a fun backdrop on the PanyKirki fairground events.

🐾 Where Jernull Finds the Wire

"I can always find a way in." -Dollar Llama, Adjacker Extraordinaire

Starved from the absence of Kenda, Jernull found himself wandering, untethered. He would wander for hours slapping at his P_ear and in a single afternoon, managed to lose his a-part-ment because of all the credit demerits he earned from shutting off his advertisements. He didn't care, nothing seemed right without Kenda. Since seeing the dead Footmen, he worried, certain she was in trouble. The world didn't make sense. He needed information. Chattering headbangers walked and waded, through product litter on the ground, alongside him slapping and tapping their P_ears, jostling him until he sought refuge in a throughway. He slumped against a wall and reasoned that he'd rather morg than take his paternal figure's place in Bits and Bytes. Worse, still, he'd rather not live without Kenda. He paired her presence in his life with a *HaloLamp!* As this thought entered his consciousness, an ad for HaloLamp! began to sing its jingle,

> *For when it can't be bright enough-*
> *Snap on a HaloLamp for extra light and stuff!*
> *Can't see at all when it's dark at night?*
> *A HaloLamp brightens your life.*

Credits started mounting in his account, and he slapped them away and he set his P_ear to full disable, which was only used if a user was undergoing surgery, he knew the codes, since he helped to develop them. Patients kept waking to accept advertisements and it made TapAlong implant surgery difficult. There were warnings and instructions about how to turn the unit back on. He slapped away the remaining warning messages. A great silence filled his mind, like a great inhalation.

For the first time since Kenda disappeared, he felt good. Nothing about his past prepared him for the release from the bindings of the constant information flow. He felt empty, but keen, ready, alert. He stood and ran his hand along the side of the building he'd been leaning on; it was sleek, but there were imperfections in the Cretemix that his fingers felt and grazed over, and as he touched each one, he felt more alive. He broke into a run, dragging his hand on the building. By the time he'd reached the other end of the throughway, his hand was raw and bloody. At the edge of the throughway, a man was regarding him with curiosity.

"Hurt yourself?"

"No, I'm fine. It's funny. I actually feel healed."

"Mmmmm." The man mused, nodding, adding, "What are you doing here?"

"I'm just—I don't know. My name is Jernull. Uh, Banburn."

"I know who you are. I see you tripped your feed."

Jernull brought his hand instinctively, protectively up to his console. "How did you know?"

"Surgical setting is an orange LED. Don't mind me. I prefer it that way, so we can talk. I've been trying to find you."

"Why?"

"You are an interesting person. I have admired your work, like your Billy story and the interest and insurance newsports you EEMed. I am very pleased to make your acquaintance finally. I'm Rassco. There are others I work with; they have watched your career with great joy."

"Those ideas and the Billy stories nearly got me thrown out of college."

"That is why they are vital works. No one throws anyone out of college for citing an advertisement."

"True. But they do carry rewards for repetition." Jernull said automatically.

"I know the old jingle, let's see, how did it go?

Earn your credits
In the old tradition
brand and tagline
Get Rewards for Repetition!"

"Uh, don't sing it. It makes me feel..."

"As it does me, but real nausea, not P_ear-fed emotion."

Jernull noted the man wore a hat that covered his P_ear. Then he realized the hat covered the absence of a P_ear. "What do you want from me?"

"I work with a group that recruits people like you. We are keenly interested in your theories and your desire to transmit information to others. We think your ideas are extraordinary. The ways you try to show them to the world is in itself, unique. Do not be deterred in your queries-a great mind always questions. The question is more important than the answer because the question, when posed rightly takes us further."

"I struggle with intersections that I cannot find. I know there is some other path I haven't explored because there are those who want to insure against my finding that path. They are betting against truth to prevent further intersections for others."

"Well put. I believe you. I work with people whose focus is gathering and revealing, but it is through the question that we hope to be conduits of truth. Our group is called MerroWire, or The Wire, for short. We want to create a new delivery method that you have hinted at in your work. Member-supported, faithful deliverance."

As understanding washed over him, Jernull felt a rush like he had never known, but he had so many questions that held him back. "I'd like to investigate what you are doing before I say yes."

"I knew you would, investigation is what we're all about. Take a listen, and decide for yourself." The man moved to the Cretewall and opened up a secret cut.

A doorway opened. Jernull cradled his bleeding hand, and followed Rassco, ducking out of the AmberRed Funlight of the waning afternoon into a well-lit passageway. As the door closed behind them it did not leave a trace on the imperfect cretemixed wall.

They slipped into a lobby with a high arch and a great hallway beyond. There were black and white markings there labeled with the words, Times New Roman. Rassco hurried them through this; Jernull would have loved to examine it, but he was too exhausted to ask Rassco to stop. Finally, they emerged into a green room.

"Take a seat. I have something earth-shattering for you." Rassco handed Jernull a folio. "These are called payprs. Our group was very pleased to get a copy of this record from a friend of yours. They have a great deal more information than this, but this strikes to the very heart of what we do. We are honored to be able to read it and get it to you. We've even arranged a meeting."

Jernull turned the folded thing over in his hand. There were markings everywhere. Several slips of paypr slipped out from the pile onto the table. Rassco helped him put it back in order and showed him how it was like a mindscreen, that he had just to read from left to right. Jernull began to read, asking questions along the way. His eyes adjusted quickly to reading this way and the words echoed in his mind, "integrity…investigation…yellow kid…" Nothing could have prepared him for what his eyes and mind consumed. After a while, he had to know.

"Who gave you this?"

Rassco smiled, and flipped the folio over and pointed to a small inscription which read, "Organic copy, sourced from Spine Archives-authenticated by RiEF."

Rassco's face beamed as he explained, "She is a Spine acolyte, an adherent to another group with a philosophy similar to ours, but she said to tell you her username used to be Harkonna 311371."

Jernull smiled. A message from her. Speaking to him in this form. He read on, hungry for the words she had sent for him. It took him a long while, and Rassco helped him with some of the words and connections. The very last page held a poem.

Information is power,
reports are gold-
But as reporters are beholden
Lies can be told then.

Speakers can turn phrases
spin a web of mis-understanding
make the masses less demanding.

Those with the questions were not heard
Bowed before the altar and were altered.
A final solid place, was not to be found
Scree on slopes, all reason, unsound.

No original source, all was jest,
A world covered in circus bread.
Full of bad reasons, disturbed
Familiar and repetitive, absurd.

And so with them, fell into decay,
The icon that could keep chaos at bay
a bell-unrung, freedom forfeit
Iron town crier, rusts in the desert.

Jernull had so many questions. He stood. He clenched his fists. His eyes had the look of someone who is trying to stare down time.

❧A Minding

"Footmen, over there." XY slid back into the throughway. "It is so important that you walk casually. Chat about product. Tug your hairstrands and tap as you used to-never mind that your P_ear is a fake. We have got to get 5 builds down and up the Pahshen Throughway. We will hopefully catch our contact at the Wire there. There only two Footmen, so that's in our favor."

"Got it."

Kenda followed XY out. She marveled at the plasmold mesh on the building, remembering the popping sound that the seam made. It reminded her of her own powerful knowledge. The boots reminded her of cruelty. As XY had told her when they set out, "The best power is one you don't have to continually exert, constant fear as the rule is cruel."

They moved around the two patrols easily and rounded the next bend. There were two DrinkCoffee! shops and four Coffee!!Coffee!! cafes here. They ducked in one to avoid another patrol. As they neared the Pashen, they ran afoul of a show patrol. It was an anomaly. Normally, Footmen were run in pairs, but a show patrol could have a hundred Footmen patrol the same block, called in the Newsports, a parade of protection. They were all heavily armed, with Heart and Mind Isolation Beams in their arms. They were scanning for something. Only Kenda and XY could guess at what that was; the rest of the people in this sector had no clue, nor did they even question. The show patrol were marching double time. Kenda tried to move back in the throughway and was caught up in a crowd of senders vidcasting the Footmen.

"Hey! Get off me!" She demanded. The crowd jostled her. Suddenly, she found herself surrounded by the crowd of Footmen. To her surprise, they barely noticed.

They chatted amongst themselves.

"Got to find her he says. She morged two agents he says."

"Been scanning for two weeks."

"No Harkonna311371 anywhere."

"We can't isolate her if we don't find her."

"Gaw. They are all looking for me. I shouldn't have come." She tried to walk casually through them. She took her hand out of her pocket to tap at her fake console. Something clattered to ground. Her feet stopped moving. She felt at her now empty pockets and twisted around only to confirm that her console key was now on the ground, being inspected by some of the gathering Footmen. She froze in the middle of the walkway.

She was stuck; she couldn't move the boots, and didn't dare take them off. XY was headed into the ranks to get her. Kenda tried to wave her off. *She'll be morged trying to save me!*

She mouthed to XY, "No, go back."

One of Footmen picked up the control key, "It's got red on it."

"They aren't red. Control keys are silver."

"It repeats, again."

"How?"

"I dunno. Just grab it."

"I already did. It isn't grey. It's got red on it."

"You said that already."

"It repeats, again."

"How?"

One of them noticed Kenda. "Hey-this is a show patrol, get out of the way."

The Footmen looked up at her. A small circle tightened about her. Two of them took her elbows and tried to turn her about to face the questioner.

"She won't move."

Kenda smiled softly and dug her toes into the liner of the boot, trying to look innocent, trying to keep from being lifted out of her boots.

"Hi..." She waved weakly.

The men at her elbows began to shift her side to side to free her from the boots.

"Farce, her boots are stuck. Mine do that too."

"Look, her feet are coming out. User, you must clear the street. We are scanning."

"This key looks like a boot key."

"Her shoes look like boots, too."

"Scan her."

One of the Footmen, saw her ankle emerging from the top of the boot, "Her ankle, holy gaw! She's S----!" He didn't get to utter another sound because an M-41 Heart and Mind isolation beam had halted his revelation and dropped him from behind.

Kenda shoved her foot back in the boot.

"Beaks fell over. Did someone friendly fire again?"

"Is he morged?"

"Did she do it?"

"She doesn't have an iso beam."

"Scan her, now!" Six Footmen waved their control key by her console. Nothing happened. It took some time to process that it wasn't responding. In that time, everything happened in very fast time for Kenda. She snatched one of the control keys being waved furiously at her head and she stumbled forward. Several more Footmen dropped, due to M-41 stunner blasts from somewhere over Kenda's shoulder. She heard XY give a low grunt and then, "Run!"

Her feet were moving! She kicked out to her right and the two closest key wavers collapsed with only mild ankle breaks. She also grabbed some keys and flung them down a CoolWalk! Trash Blower Grate. Some Footmen were catching on, but they were busy requesting, via EEM, how to respond to this unscannable unit and violent user.

XY had cut through finally and pushed into Kenda, "Run! Don't forget to kick!"

The Footmen were thawing from their inaction, with instructions,

"Banburn says to record a vid."

"Says to beamcuff first, though."

"No, beamcuff after vid."

Kenda and XY had made it near the edge of the show patrol, when they both smashed into Obur, a sizable Footmen, who seemed no worse for the collision. They bounced off in a v shape, landing hard on the surfacewalk.

"Hoof." Kenda lost her breath. She had taken his elbow to the face.

"Ack. Our units." XY pointed out that their P_ears were on the ground, indicating somewhere in Obur's shadow.

The shock from this new turn of events, an unscannable unit, a trail of dazed Footmen on the ground, and now, P_ear units cleanly disconnected from user's heads broke many a train of thought that day.

Then, a firm command blared from the external speaker of the units on the Footmen, "Get them!" accompanied by their vid-captured photos that one Footmen had EEMed at Banburn's request.

Every head in the vicinity turned toward them. XY and Kenda scrambled to their feet.

Obur said, "Get who?"

Footmen feet shuffled toward them. XY's stolen Iso Beam was out of reach having been subsumed under the press of the patrol.

XY and Kenda cast about for exit routes and found none. Kenda caught sight of the glint from her P_ear unit on the ground.

Kenda pointed to the units and shouted, "Recover the cover! Recover the cover!"

That command, they knew. It was the primary mandate for all Footmen. Keep the units safe. Carriers were secondary. "Recover the cover, cap the carrier," as they say.

In the scuffle to recover the covers, Kenda and XY pushed through to the edge, taking many blows to the head and jabs to the ribs. Finally, they emerged from the crush of bodies.

Obur was just outside the throng. He slammed his meaty paws down hard on XY's shoulder, swinging her round and caught Kenda up by the waist. They both thrashed in his grip, aiming with their boots to do maximum damage. He managed to keep their kicks out of reach.

Kenda smashed against Obur with her fist. The console key she was gripping poked her palm. She stared at it for a second, then she waved it at his console. It did not open. She notched the key into her fingers and jimmied the side of the console open. Blood creased out of the sides from the contact points. Obur gave a jerk and flung XY down. He squeezed Kenda until she thought her ribs would implode. Kenda tried to reach for the console again, but her air ways slowing being cut off, as Obur tightened his hold with the free hand. Suddenly, the world went sideways and Kenda tumbled to the ground. Next to her, Obur had also dropped. He gagged in pain. Kenda could see the white bones of his leg craning out of his grey uniform, which was slowly pulsing with blood from the wound. XY's favored kick always managed to find the knee joints from the side.

"Give me your hand." She yanked Kenda up to standing. Both of their faces were spattered in blood. Behind them, Footmen tussled over the covers, they were worth a great deal of credits. There external speakers blared with an agonized scream.

Kenda and XY took off down the next build and onto the throughway that would take them to the Pashen. XY kept looking back to see if they were followed. She saw nothing but a stray Push on the way. She found the secret cut that she was looking for, and soon, she and Kenda were safe inside the front entrance of the MerroWire, face to face with a friendly, grinning man named Rassco. "You must be Kes' why? Is this the Kenda? Or is it the other way around."

XY laughed. "Yes, this is the Kenda. You must have gotten the message and the folio that we sent earlier and you were you able to find him?"

"I did. He is the one that described the beautiful sienna face of Kenda to me." Kenda's face warmed. Rassco continued, "You have great timing. How did you avoid that mob out there? I want to know all the details. The system is lighting up with vids of it. What a mess. You are amazing. No time now, though. Get inside." Rassco pushed the door in and closed it behind them. "Make yourself comfortable. I'll send someone to get you soon." Rassco bowed and trotted off.

They both took a seat in the lobby hall. It was painted black and white, with iron works everywhere. But the arch over their heads had lines and overlapping lines that covered nearly the whole ceiling. Kenda looked closer and saw that they were words. *So many, hundreds, thousands?* The printed word never ceased to delight Kenda. She and XY spent the next half hour waiting for Jernull, reading the arches, columns and walls in the hall. They spoke of every subject. RiEF would be beside herself. There was a section that talked about the fallen, with a plaque that read, "For those who gave their lives in search of truth, the only answer is more questions."

The Pair

A woman with red and black streaked, platinum-blond hair walked in where they stood. She looked like an ancient mythic warrior, that Kenda often sourced pictures of when reading the old stories. She had black knee-high boots and a curious triangular contraption on her back. She introduced herself as Hadorn the Harleeqin.

"Glad to meet you, Kes why, Kenda."

"Your walls are so-" Kenda sought a word worthy of the room and the monument, "so profound."

Hadorn nodded, "I love this room. Anything that sanctifies truth can only serve truth."

XY asked, "You serve truth?"

"The Wire does, and I serve the Wire. Rassco has gathered everyone for you. He sends his apologies, but he was sending out scouts to enable your escape. Come with me." She brought them back to the conference room and with a flourish, tapped a code on the wall, making an opening in the wall. Kenda and XY passed through the door panel and stood in the huge well-lit room.

Like a man slapped from sleep, Jernull whipped his head around. The sight of Kenda hit Jernull hard. He was already tearing up from reading the folio spread before him, but now he rushed to her, hunched down to meet her face and took her chin in his hands, checking for injuries, running his hand over her P_ear removal scars.

"I'm fine, Jernull. I'm great." She assured him, laughing a bit with joy to see him. She noted the folio spread on the table and knew instantly why he looked upset.

He hugged her. "I thought—you were—I kept—I mean your feed kept showing morg codes—how?"

He pulled back from the embrace and stared at her; he could hardly believe she was standing in front of him. She said to him, "Jernull, I think you'd better sit down. It's going to be a bit of a story."

"I can't believe you're here. I saw the dead Footmen, which seems to be part of it from what Rassco has told me was in the message that err—Cause y sent."

XY corrected, "It's pronounced Kes' why."

"Right. Lovely name and sentence fragment. Tell me everything. Rassco's group says that a RiEF sent over details on a plan that folds nicely with what the Wire wants to do."

XY nodded. "Yes, we do. It hasn't passed yet, but I know it will. I feel it. "

Rassco smiled broadly, "We have similar mandates to yours-we are dedicated to story, too, but we call ours, The Leed."

🐾The Minding

Kenda recounted the parts of her story that she was conscious during, and XY filled in the rest. Jernull took it all in, nodding and asking questions, as was his way.

Jernull looked at XY in awe. "I admire your dedication. It would be easy to stay hidden in your position. I think I have seen you before."

XY laughed and shared a look with Kenda, about something they had theorized a while ago, "I think you used me as your inspiration for your lead 'running woman' in your Billy Story. You might have seen me on one of my run-ins a while back with the WalkingMen. Kenda told me."

Jernull was floored, "That was you? I should have helped you."

"You are now. Speaking of which, we have much to plan and little time to do it. Let's get to it." They discussed getting back to the stronghold. Rassco had lots to offer on that front. They also hammered out the details for The Wire's next move and how it could support the Lighthouse plan. Once they had assigned roles and timing, XY and Rassco left the room so Kenda could speak alone with Jernull. Hadorn, who had been silently taking down the plan details from the corner of the room that she was responsible for executing, had also found somewhere else to be.

When they were alone, Jernull held both of Kenda's hands.

"This plan is the right thing to do; I know it."

"I think so, too. It won't be easy. What exactly did Rassco mean when he said that he thought that there will be Dropcore there? What are they like? I didn't understand this idea of power amplified."

"I've only seen one once at my Paternal's building. They are Footmen, but an upper-echelon force. He had a red band on his right wrist. The plans for them had very simple P_ears, which means they get their orders directly from my paternal alone. Like most Footmen, the Dropcore also carry M-41 Heart and Mind

Isolation beams, but unlike them, the ones the Dropcore carry don't have a stun setting, they only have a kill setting."

"Oh my gaw. Is there any way to stop them?"

"I've never tried. Rassco and I think they can be called off with a code from the main console in my paternal's office. That is the part of the plan where Hadorn is going with me to hack that console. Remember to meet me at the lighthouse entrance, after you get the signal and do your job, right?"

"I will."

"One more thing...I—I..."

Kenda sensed he was fumbling. She helped him. "No need to thank me. I know what it means to need understanding."

"..." Jernull's face flushed red. He dropped his eyes and his fading azure bangs fell predictably to cover most of his deep red blushed cheeks.

Kenda held his face with her hands and they touched foreheads.

Hadorn came noisily in the room. She looked at the floor, coughed and readjusted the device on her back. "XY asked me to come get you."

Jernull opened his eyes.

Kenda stepped away from him and slipped out of the room. She headed down the hallway. Hadorn ran after her and pulled her aside, and said, "If the Spine move forward with the plan, I will come see if I can help you at the lighthouse, after I help Jernull. I hope you will come to see how faithful we are to the word."

"I already do. I read the arches while we waited. They were astounding. How will you and Jernull get by the Footmen?"

Hadorn patted the device on her back. "I've got help from the ancients. I built it myself."

"What is that thing? Don't you all use Footmen boots?"

"Some do. When we can get them. I prefer this. It is a modified crossbow. I got the idea from the baggers. It fires a magnetic plasmold net that fuses the Footmen boots together. It is non-lethal, but it takes hours to remove. We use them to aid our escape, when we are out gathering stories."

"Gaw. You *are* as dedicated to the word as Spine are."

"Our commitment is the same. Only our source is different; our stories are the current, the now, the present. Our stories are the moment. We seek is the Leed. It is elusive, there are many false leeds. Banburn wants to keep our Leeds from infiltrating the newsports. Because of this some have died for the Leed. If this plan works both of our stories can be shared."

Kenda looked keenly at this woman. Her eyes shone with the fire in Kenda's own soul. Source and Leed meant the same thing, helping others to see clearly, and Kenda marveled again at how powerful a force understanding is.

"Good night and good luck, Kenda. Until we meet again."

Kenda grinned. It wasn't nighttime, but this was a traditional Wire farewell. XY and she had read about it in the lobby. Kenda nodded to Hadorn, saying, "All things flow from Source."

"Oh, wait. I wanted to ask you something. Why do you use hair color even in these walls? You don't have a brandsponsor."

Hadorn tossed her platinum-blond, red and black streaked locks, "No." She laughed, "I just like it." Then, she turned and ran back to get Jernull and get prepped for the mission.

Kenda smiled. She watched Hadorn retreat and then she turned back and followed the beautiful words on the wall as they led her on to the Arches lobby. She collided with XY.

"Whoa! Gaw! There you are. Did you see Hadorn? She wanted to speak to you."

"I did. She's insane! Did she show you the crossbow?!"

"Yes, I mean, yes she's insane, and yes, she showed me the crossbow! I bet you two could revise the Spine Archives on tenacity! Listen, we've got to go. Rassco says the show patrol isn't near our minding mission. He also gave me some info on where Dayzee might be on the day of the pageant, if her patterns hold up."

Kenda's breath hitched. She looked at XY and tried to hold back tears. "Please, let me go early with QRoSe and try to help her."

"I'll make sure of it. Now let's get out of her before the Show Patrols come back, or worse ones with Dropcore in it."

"I'm ready."

"I'll bet you have a great deal of emotional knowledge to share with RiEF when we get back."

"I've sourced that a woman never tells. "

"Not even for the Archive?"

Kenda rolled her eyes and pulled XY out to the doorpanel that led to the throughway. "Let's get to the minding." They changed quickly back into their disguises, but this time, Kenda hung the control key around her neck, inside her massive purple frilled top. They crept out of the door panel, wary of what might wait on the other side, but Rassco's men did a great job of cloaking that area in a very dark Funlight.

XY admired this use, "Rassco's got style, smart way to use the system like this."

They sprinted down the throughway. They made it easily to the place that the calendrix indicated their subject would be. XY explained on the way that this was the first minding that would involve disabling the Emotional Transfer Grid first. ABie and RiEF did the leg work on that. It was simple. A data packet severed the connection. It had only to be waved near the P_ear, until the LED light registered the packet by flashing blue twice. They had already located their target and done this earlier in the week. The plan was to leave the connections to undo themselves, gradually so as not to draw the attention of the Footmen, but to get back to the target before that could happen.

XY and Kenda found the girl weeping in a corner by the Hairstrand upgrade center. According to her calendrix, she was supposed to be selling bottles of spray that made hair glow in the dark when EEMs arrived. There was a full box of it on her lap. She did not seem interested in the least by her launch products.

XY approached first, "Are you Jova?"

The girl nodded. Tears streamed her dirty face. She was of medium build and she looked like she hadn't slept well in days. She had a tattered blue shawl indicating a low-level of Sympaticouch sponsorship. There was a great deal of scarring around her P_ear that made Kenda's stomach turn.

"XY said, "Kenda, stay with her. Tell her what you can. I'm going to sweep around the block for Footmen." XY ducked away to scout the perimeter. Kenda told Jova to use credits to order dimmer Funlights. Carnival Dusk flickered on. Kenda thought, *My sentiments exactly*.

Kenda said, "Hello, Jova. I am Kenda. That was XY. She's all business, but she's kind. We want to help you, but I don't know how you'll take what I am about to tell you. Have you ever felt lost? Do you feel like your friends aren't really saying anything to you, even though you have been EEMing with them all day? Do you remember diagnostics? Do you remember the pain?"

Jova looked up at Kenda, "Yes. To most of that. Especially that last one. It happened right after I tried to find out how I could disconnect my P_ear. I don't want it anymore. I got three diagnostics that day, each one worse than the last. What is wrong with me? Why is this happening? Why do you know what's wrong with me? What's going on with my P_ear? The Dollar Llama keeps adjacking it. I'm only here because I got a message on my calendar to meet with someone to fix my credits; I am shy this month."

Kenda sat down next to her. "What I am going to tell you is going to be strange at first, but it is true, and you should attempt to find that out for yourself anyway, but for now, just listen. I was once like you."

❦ Full Circle

With Jova settled in the stronghold, Kenda and XY left to get dressed for the circle. They left Jova, eating something that QRoSe had cooked up (that probably included carrots), and chatting happily with ABie. They would listen to the circle remotely and record it for the Archives.

In the wide meeting room, there was a packed house. All around, members shifted in their benches and murmured solemnly.

XY would speak second as Speaker for the Dissent, whose job it was to give an alternate proposal to current operating mode. The Speaker for the Status Quo's job, was to state the current course and objections to the dissenting view. It was a formality to put the discussions out there because keeping information from information guardians was next to impossible; they had access to every source. Everyone here knew why they were here.

The Speaker for the Status Quo, C'Dia, stepped forward and addressed the circle. "Protectors of Source,"

The crowd responded, "from which all things flow."

"We are here to vote on the Lighthouse Plan. We have offered our new allies, The Wire, the opportunity to assist us if we vote to move forward, and they have accepted. Jernull has joined them."

A murmur rippled through the crowd. XY beamed. They had not yet heard that Jernull had been found and recruited. His Billy Stories were legend in the Stronghold, not for their complexity, but for their truth.

C'Dia held up a hand and continued, "The question at hand is yes or no for that plan. The status quo is to keep maintaining the Archives and to continue our service as the guardians we were entrusted to be. This includes our continued transformative initiative to get new acolytes from the minding missions, but it does not include a mandate to initiate the wider population. Those in favor of keeping things as they are, fear that the Lighthouse Plan will endanger not only Spine members, but it could lead to the obliteration of Source itself."

The crowd knew this was part of it, and stayed as stone.

"I will now yield the floor to XY, Speaker for the Dissent."

There were mixed responses from the crowd, encouraging clapping in some groups, while hard faces and stalwart reservation glared from factions in the back corners.

XY stepped forward and waited for the tide to calm. "I would like to open this dissent opinion with news that you all probably already know. It is hard to keep things from data miners." There was a pleasant response from the members; smiles and nods moved through the room. "Here is what I know. The first is that our Kenda carrying my own XY-derivate, as nearly all of you know, has successfully sourced and just recently assimilated all her material. This is without any dilution or alteration of the original. Perfect sourcing." There was cheering at this by nearly everyone, even though it just confirmed what they already knew.

"Kenda and I have just come back from a Minding, where we used the data packet that ABie and RiEF developed, to disable the Emotional Transfer Grid before we brought the new acolyte in for sourcing. Her name is Jova, and she sourced beautifully, just like Kenda."

Nods of approval and whispers rounded the room. XY continued, "We have waited so long to master that perfect transfer and we now see that the key is to disrupt the Emotional Transfer Grids in new recruits before introducing Source. It is the only way that the information acclimates when both emotional and intellectual systems are working in concert with each other. At long last, Source can conceivably be safely replicated without error, forever."

The meeting room bellowed to life and most Spine jumped to their feet. The standing ovation made Kenda and RiEF blush. XY was stoic, as always. Kenda's hand nearly went to the side of her head, but she stopped it midway, and used it to wipe the tears from her face.

XY raised her hand, and the applause died down. The Spine resettled on their benches, as she continued.

"Since our acquisition of the lighthouse, we've been busy. Our repair crews have oiled every gear and pulley, it is pristine again, the inside at least, just like we planned, Source be praised. I know we had intended to use the lighthouse as expanded storage, but it may prove its worth as an as even greater instrument than we intended. The lighthouse will also finally bring light, as it originally intended."

Kenda wasn't sure that QRoSe's wordplay that she'd inserted in the speech here was appropriate, but XY trusted her and loved the light metaphor so much, so it was left in.

"We have longed for the day that would afford us the opportunity to serve the wider population again. I say that our time is upon us, now. I see in Kenda a tide change in the world. The Ghdess has spoken new words. I know that you must have all Sourced them by now. This new mandate from her has been interpreted by most of us as a new direction. But it is Kenda that finally made the necessary connections. We are Spine. We are the back and the bone, the protection, the keepers." XY paused to let this settle in. She needed this metaphor to wash over them.

"But to safeguard is not to withhold. We were never meant to keep the world thirsty. We were made custodians, entrusted with Source as keepers, but not guards. The irony of our guardianship is that of access for all, not just a select few. We have become guardians, not by choice, but as our past dictated. Our service in defense of Source has not been in vain, if we act now to restore it to the world. All the generations of Spine before us and the Consorcium before them have sacrificed and died for this moment. I believe they hid because they felt that one day they would be able to serve again as stewards. This is the new plan for the lighthouse. We must give everything back. We have sufficient DNA and organic paypr copies. The next chapter for the Spine is to return to our true service."

"This change could be seeded and nurtured with the proper timing. If we wait, we may have to scar both our eyes and bind our hands for all the good we will have done. We have an opportunity here- a ready audience of millions, and the event which will be vidcast to millions more. If we vote yes for this new plan, we will help this blind, insensate world emerge from its social and intellectual cocoon. We will help it rejoin the human conversation."

Several heads in the darkened room could be seen nodding, faces calm. There were others, still and unmoving.

A voice came from the far corner. It was a member with short-cropped, deep brown hair. She had two streaks of grey that framed her face. Her name was MNOla. She was one of the oldest members of Spine, and she was the most vocal opponent of the new lighthouse plan. "May I offer something to discourse?"

XY waved C'Dia off; she would allow it. To MNOla, she said the proper wording for the Request to add Discourse, "It would please me, MNOla."

"This plan is dangerous. It is a full reveal of ourselves and our purpose. *That* can only serve to target us for further Footmen patrols. The information that XY brought back from The Wire confirms the existence of the new Dropcore. They told us they were designed to find us. This kind of public exposure could ruin us. Humanity will come around. They will eventually seek something more, which will mean more minding missions. More important though, than my duty to my fellow members is my calling to Source. If we are not here to protect it, it will be lost forever."

Kenda knew MNOla well. She had had many debates with her in the grow rooms about this very thing. She also knew that her greatest passion would be the very place to reference here. XY signaled her.

Kenda stepped forward, "I request to reply to discourse."

XY nodded, "It would please me to hear, Kenda."

Kenda spoke with passion, "With all due respect to MNOla, we'd all like to think that humanity can by themselves fight their way out of their stupor, and think their way into new course of action, but the reality is that without help, the pull will win. It is too strong."

"We all know the silence of the room within a room, and we've all been tempted and tested in the Platitudes. Breaking into the silence requires the resistance of screens. I have never felt more alive than when I could listen to my own thoughts without interruption. When I could decide my fate and my direction without being juiced with emotion for a product or expected to like something or endorse something. This never would have happened without the words to build that around me. Words have enabled me to experience a thousand lifetimes in my own mind-to test a thousand different directions. And to express what I know to others. This power to be able wield words is not to be underestimated, not even by those who are so intimate with that knowledge that they have lost sight of what it means not to have it. Everyone should know the difference between rage and outrage."

"Through the Archives, I have told you about the horror of the network broadcast tower. The Push, the Twitch-how there is still life there that gets bagged and shipped. You have all read the statements that I made for the Archives. You know all this and more. If you vote to withhold that from humanity, you are consigning them to the Footmen forever. The new words from the Ghdess weren't a new direction. They were the Spine mandate all along. Somewhere lost in the explosion and the release of the spores that killed the trees, we lost our way, couldn't see the forest for the lack of trees. The Spine chose to focus only on protecting. The sharing is equally important. Seeds must be sown. Books must have a reader."

MNOla put her hand to her heart. "The reader is more sacred than Source?"

All eyes turned to Kenda. The room hung on the edge of this question.

Kenda looked around. She knew the answer; she just needed the conviction, and the right metaphor. Her dream came to her.

"When the world lost Source, the digitals were losing information, but that wasn't the only thing lost. Interest went toward the visual and the audio. Vids fed them everything that they thought they needed, but Source is nothing without a reader."

A heated excited conversation rippled through the room. They hushed, when Kenda began to speak again.

"Source and reader. When they pair, they become a third thing-understanding, someone in the dining hall called it aufheben. It is the dialectic. When there is no one left to give a story to, Source flow stops. Without this river, all that is left is a drought of human conversation."

Kenda pointed toward the main entrance of the stronghold, "Your *readers* are out there."

The room was quiet. Heads tilted in thought, eyes rolled to the ceiling. A few Spine were weeping. Conversations rolled excitedly around the room.

MNOla's expression changed, her face slackened. She seemed physically struck. She managed something akin to acceptance to flood her face and she said, "I yield my vote. Kenda has spoken truly."

The wash of excitement moved through the room like a hurricane. Clapping began in spurts and several factions leapt to their feet, urging others, until the entire room was on its feet, roaring and applauding.

XY waited, as Kenda received her due. She raised her hand slowly, "I feel like we have reached a consensus. As Speaker for the Dissent, I have to call a vote. Will any call second in favor of the lighthouse plan?"

"I call a second." A woman with eyes like grey flint, put her hand in the air. "I trained with MNOla and I shared her concerns, but if we do not face the Footmen, we cannot ask others to do so in our place. I, Talemi 020.92, second this motion."

XY smiled, she hadn't needed Kenda to second it after all. She thought, "Talemi and MNOla had endorsed it! That would carry the day. Kenda won them over." XY had been trained by both of those ancient women. Their love of Source and their conviction at this moment, even in their resistance touched her. She could see how it touched everyone else in the room, as well. She thought it very fitting that they should be the key voices in this decision. "We have a second. All in favor of this resolution?"

Every voice rang out, "Aye, by the scribe."

"Are there any opposed?"

Not one black cloak stirred in the meeting hall. The hush was palpable. Heads turned, worried, expectant eyes sought movement. The shift in their purpose awaited the passing of this moment. The fate of their lives hinged on it.

The tension blew from the room as a relieved XY bowed her head and said, "It is passed. We will use the lighthouse to bring light once more."

🐦 Daybreak and the Break of Day

"I think the best business model is a monthly payment plan." -B. Banburn, EEM to graduating class, Banburn U

"The MissInfo pageant award is for how much information you put out. It doesn't matter what the info is, just how much and how often. I much and I often." - Blanca Rudio, EEM after winning MissInfo Award for Excellence in quantity in Newsporting.

On the morning of the MissInfo Pageant, there were patches of weird light being thrown around. Many of the SOLARFLAIR wave panels were malfunctioning, courtesy of the Wire's virus. As a result, true sunlight filtered in, no longer transformed by the artificial wave filters, but a pure reckoning of heat and light, the yellow star in her true gown.

The heat touched the faces of those in attendance and they blinked profusely. Some stopped on the COOLWALK! and stared up in awe. The sudden heat vaporized the last of the scheduled, manufactured rainfall, which sizzled and dissipated. A thick humidity made itself felt and settled down amongst the crowd.

On the stage, the Miss Information candidate, Kitty Reed, shifted uncomfortably in her raincoat-themed bikini. She had been dressed for the scheduled light mist and now the last of it hung in the humid air. The rain had been evaporated by the sudden appearance of actual sunlight, making her yellow rain cap, blue raindrop hair print overlay, which pulsed with nano-particulates emulating rainfall, ludicrously out of nature's new plan.

Kenda headed toward the fairgrounds via throughways with QRoSe, who, despite her size, could almost become invisible. They had cloaked their hair so that it matched another insignificant sponsor. They moved swiftly and warily; Footmen were always around.

In one of the throughways that emptied out in a smaller city center, they came to a small DrinkMOR café. They had information from the Wire that Dayzee was going to be doing a product release here. They found her.

She stood, swaying in place. Her hair was askew and only moderately colored, fading between upgrades. Her right eye was wide and bulging, and her left eye was half-closed. She turned at the sound of their approach and looked Kenda square in the eye.

"Kitty, Kitty Reed?" Her hand went to her P_ear console, but didn't make it all the way there. Her fingers tapped the air in a sick pantomime, hanging in mid-air.

"Dayzee?"

"Shugso! I drink it on my COOLWALK! and when I go out, I drink it when I am walking on my SYMPAti-cofunlight is the cool Popeularutty!!! It feels with you and next to youandwon't let you…won't let me…"

"Dayzee? Talk to me!"

"Won't let you…" Dayzee pounded her fist in her right eye, bringing forth a dribble of blood.

Kenda gasped. "Help me QRoSe!" They grabbed Dayzee's arms and put them down at her sides gently, but firmly. QRoSe staunched the blood with a bandage she produced from a side pocket of her clothes. She wrapped it around Dayzee's head and tied it off.

Dayzee paid no notice. She lifted her arm and tapped furiously on her P_ear unit in a pattern that perplexed Kenda. She saw it to be the surgical shut off mode, because Dayzee's LED was flashing orange, but she kept repeating the sequence over and over and over. Her P_ear issued an audible warning-
"…this shutoff mode, done repeatedly could damage substrate systems and matrices."

"Kitty, please. Help me find my Shugso. It'ssssu -per…" She sputtered and was quiet.

Another external P_ear speaker announcement emanated from Dayzee's implant…

"Your unit is in need of an upgrade, please remain absolutely still, Footmen have been dispatched to your location."

Something familiar flashed in Dayzee's eyes, something akin to recognition and she touched Kenda's shoulder lightly. She sputtered, "pair danger…pair danger…pair danger…" Dayzee's good eye locked with Kenda's eyes and her fingers dug into Kenda's shoulders. She seemed desperate to convey something. There was a wild, animal need there, her entire face contorted in pain.

This moment of clarity quickly passed and was replaced by a look of fear. Her arms fell slack at her side.

QRoSe said, "We have to do something quickly and get out of here. The Footmen are coming."

"I know, but what?" she looked back again at Dayzee and put her palm against her left cheek.

"Dayzee, you have to stop slapping that pattern. It's going to morg you. Day, can you hear me?"

"QRoSe, I can't leave her like this." Dayzee jerked violently as though she'd received a shock, her body arched backwards, went bolt upright, and then, she was still again. Kenda's hand felt singed and warm. She tried to wave the control key, but the console didn't open.

"Day!" Kenda burned with rage and her throat choked with sorrow. She was crying profusely and trying to dab the blood that had trickled out of the makeshift bandage and down Dayzee's face. Kenda pulled her arm and tried to get her to move. She wasn't at Push yet, so she wasn't moving.

She waved the control key again, frantically. An audible snick sounded.

"Wha-?" Kenda looked at the console which had lifted slightly at the edge. She pried the console open. Several of the connections were entirely black. QRoSe looked over Kenda's shoulder.

"Oh my. I actually have seen this. An early acolyte had it."

"What do we do?"

QRoSe took a modified P_ear unit from her cloak fold. She tapped in a distress call. It went out under a secret user channel that the Spine used. "If they can get here in time, they can pick up Dayzee. Let me see if I can disable or reset the alarm. That might hold off the Footmen."

QRoSe worked to disconnect the alarms. She unwound some of the Emotional Transfer Grid connections, but they had established very deep roots. She passed the Transfer Grid Release packet over it, but doubted it would work at a system this torqued. Kenda smoothed Dayzee's hair out of her wound and spread some healing sealant on it from her bag.

"Day? Dayzee?

Dayzee's eyes fluttered. Her lips parted, "P_ear Danger. Pair danger Shhh-shh, beware, brown hair, run, run, run-CoolWalk is fun, fun, fun..." Her eyes narrowed and she seemed to focus again on Kenda, trying to force understanding by sheer will.

Kenda whispered, "What Day? Help me, help you. What do we do? Can you move?" Dayzee's head lolled and then propped itself upright. She pursed her lips and was still again.

Kenda spoke softly to her. "I'm here Dayz, I'm gonna help you." She watched QRoSe's capable hands nip and remove strands, a few at a time. Soon, QRoSe cradled her prize in her cinnamon-colored hands. It was a smooth metal oval. "It may still track locations."

"What can we do with it to throw them off... Maybe we can smash it? I'll throw it on a nearby tram, I guess, but *we* still need to be able to track her—oh, Gaw! A bagger-run!"

A Bagger Tram came to a stop behind them. Kenda whirled around and her eyes grew huge. "No! You are not taking her!" QRoSe stepped up to match Kenda's defensive line. They were rigid and stoic in the direct beamlight from the tram, which temporarily blinded both of them.

Behind them, Dayzee was swaying and absently touching the place that her P_ear had just occupied. She smiled, ever so slightly.

Kenda and the formidable QRoSe clutched their boot console keys in their closed palms, and they stood fast between the tram and Dayzee.

"Kenda, run. Get to the lighthouse to do your duty to Source. I can take one Bagger, and get Dayzee out."

"I am not leaving either of you."

The tram lights wavered as the Bagger stepped out. They strained to make out what was coming at them. A single Footman boot with the Dropcore red stripe down the side dropped into view behind the tram door.

"Dropcore? We won't get close enough to use the boots on this one. We'll be iso'ed. Get out of here, Kenda."

Kenda was frozen. She watched in gaping horror as the driver slid around the door. The tramlights blinded her and she blinked her eyes and put her hand up in defiance to stave off the glare.

She refocused and faced her assailant, ready for whatever came next.

A grinning, fully-armed Hadorn stepped out into view. "How do you like my ride?"

"Hadorn! What the farce? You scared me to death! QRoSe, this is Hadorn. She is one of The Wire, XY briefed you on. She loves investigation more than you love puns."

QRoSe's bent arms slackened just the tiniest bit. Her face surveyed Hadorn critically. She was dressed in a black and gold Bagger Uni and her hair was dyed a dozen different colors, with her typical platinum blond base. It was a twelve-pack nano application, twelve dyes for a dozen brandsponsors. She had her crossbow, a plasmold weapon, a quiver of plasmold net units, and an M-41 Heart and Mind Iso Beam, set to stun. She also had a knife at her knee, just in case. She loved Nursree rhymes-took them quite literally, apparently.

"Anybody call for a lift?"

"You got the distress call?"

"I did. XY had us help monitor and provide security for today. Is this Dayz?"

"Dayzee, yes. Can you get her out of here?"

"No problem. Is she Move?"

"Push?"

"Yes, is that what you call it? Poor girl. How far along is she? I know someone who is good with them. Brings them around, sometimes."

"Oh my gosh, that's amazing. We have so much to learn. Yes, please, take her anywhere safe. I'll find her when we're done."

Hadorn shouldered her crossbow. She approached Dayzee with a calm grace. There was a tenderness to her usual violent movements. She took Dayzee's other hand and Kenda helped with the other side. Dayzee was allowing herself to be moved for the time being. She roused bit as they loaded her in the tram and secured her in with a belt. Hadorn closed the tram door. "I got it. Get on with it. I'll drop her, help Jernull, then we'll meet you down there." Hadorn smiled, revealing multi colored-harlequin teeth that matched her hair. Kenda rolled her eyes, but she knew this was just Hadorn's own will and style, and not because she needed credits. It lifted her spirits though; she let hope enter her heart that everything might not go badly today. "I can't ever repay you Hadorn."

"Vigilance be your watchword. Now, get thee gone!" Hadorn jumped in the tram.

QRoSe clapped her hand to her mouth in near glee at the pun. Kenda cracked a smile and said, "She is going to be unbearable if she ever gets access to the Archives on the Bard of Avon."

Kenda leaned down and looked in on Dayzee. The blood on her cheeks had dried. There was a calm about her face that seemed like a still pool. "I'll find you. You are in good hands with Hadorn. She is going to see if we can help you."

Dayzee muffled something like an answer and her eyes closed.

QRoSe tugged at Kenda's shoulder, "The tracker that MerroWire gave us is reading that the show patrol is one build over."

Kenda reached over Dayzee and briefly clasped Hadorn's hand. She took a last look at Dayzee and then turned her whole self toward Source's purpose and ran down the throughway behind QRoSe. The tram sped off in the other direction.

Back at the MissInfo Pageant, the true sun was having an unexpected effect on the Coolwalk! The walkway had been baking for a few hours now by the relentless glare of the solar goddess. Its viscous substrates were oozing and melting, never having known heat like this. This caused the upper layers to slide off, revealing the flat metal panels underneath. Stripped of their gelatinous outer layer, the shining panels reflected the world around in glorious near-perfect reproduction. They were extremely flat panels and without the warp of lesser metals, like the Meerers around the city. People gathered in wonder to behold themselves, reflected truly, for the very first time.

It was this preoccupation which allowed many of the Spine to enter the grounds, unnoticed at first, gathering in the center green of the Kirki Pany Fairgrounds. The black-cloaked women did not immediately catch the attention of the human throng of headbangers. The senders were mechanically tapping away at their consoles to send chirps about this new yellow Funlight that was burning their eyes and snapping quickvids of their lacerated, scarred visages in the Coolwalk! below their feet. They kept hoping to cop some credits, but Funlight had only sponsored positive remarks and for now the light was blinding them. Their reflections horrified them, and they could find no words to describe or pair their emotions to product-so silence won the day.

The crowds began to notice the women in the center of the park.

The Spine had formed a ring, gathering about the Center Green. The painted space in the middle was a cleared, green surface meant to simulate a grassy park of bygone days. This was before Coolwalk! invented pay-per-use sidewalkways that *"enhanced the user experience"*. No one really used this space because it really didn't offer any enhanced experiences or credits.

The Spine threw back their hoods. Their brown locks were immediately swirled up in the Coolwalk! vented breeze. The brown-haired mavens stood in stark contrast to the crush of a rainbow-haired populace.

Coursing through the crowds in hot pursuit, the Dropcore came to a halt in front of the ring of Spine. They were momentarily thunderstruck by the number of women standing there. Few of them had ever seen more than one or two Spine in their lifetimes and here were a mass of these mythical women, subjects of so much talk and deadly stories. Warnings from jumped memories of the Nursuree rhymes rang in their heads—

"Beware the Brown Hair!,
murderers, thieves, knives at their knees!
Natch! the Brown Hair!
They kill and they deceive
With lies that they weave."

The Dropcore Footmen didn't stay dazed for long. They had been trained for this. They began to sift closer toward the circle. There was a disturbance on the outer rim, as a bagger tram tried to press through. No one noticed. Neither did they move out of the way. The crowd could only stare slack-jawed. Some had the presence of mind to send live vidCasts that went racing across cyberspace. Millions of EEMs came flooding back trying to authenticate the rumors about the Spine being at the pageant. There were long gaps in the send/receive times, the system was overloading as 100 million P_ears fired back and forth at each other tapping their consoles furiously and hitting resend like demons possessed.

When the Spine finally brought their circle full, they numbered 330, a fraction of Spine in hiding, but the old guard was well-represented here in their numbers. MNOla and Talemi stood hand in hand. The scar they bore under their left eye, glistened in the morning light. Somewhere on their bodies there was another mark, a tattoo that went as deep as their DNA. The second that they joined hands, they had committed a crime.

The heads of P_ear Users in attendance blared with an Area - wide announcement:

Public announcement brought to you by: SHUGSO-THE SODA
OF COOL POPularity: FEEL THE LOVE WITH SHUGSO!
"Corporation Law 3902.94 says that any group numbering over 100,

joined by any body part shall be considered a danger, a crime punishable by death if it is done without prior brandsponsorship or is the work of a known state-defined terror group."

Several users tapped their consoles to request clarification, and got this response:

P_ear Core Law definitions proudly brought to you by SUGSO-THE SODA OF COOL POPularity: FEEL THE LOVE WITH SHUGSO!, "...terror groups are any group not sanctioned or sponsored by a brandcorporation, or have unknown intent...." end definition. Get SHUGSO's new suggested taglines downloaded today!

Making their way through the crowd, the Dropcore drew in closer. The Spine stood still. The only motion came from their hair and their paper-thin cloaks. Both were flying madly in the new wind blowing from the ducts attempting to cool the heat from the first sun to shine through in generations.

Shoving through the crowd toward the Center Green, was a lone bagger. The crowd was tightly packed. The rainbow-haired bagger was using elbows, but not making much headway. She occasionally cursed and may have harmlessly netted people who exerted a more spirited resistance to her getting through.

In the Center Green, each Footman raised his weapon, shouted the standard Murander oath,

"Crimeoffenders, you will be arrested if you surrender now, morged if you refuse!"

The women of the Spine did not move.

Someone shouted from the crowd, "Hey, that's like that Billy story! The running men did the same thing."

"Oh Gaw? What happened in that episode? Didn't they all get like Sympaticouches or something?" Credits flashed in several resends of this conversation.

"This is your last chance. Put your hands in the air to show surrender."

Nothing. The crowd shifted uneasily.

"Turn and SURRENDER!"

It was MNOla who spoke. "We are Spine. You all can witness that it is not we who disturb the peace. We are here to share. We are here to right an ancient imbalance. To free you. We are here to free ourselves from a time when we let fear cast away our purpose. The gift we offer is a glimpse from a million windows. To see yourselves better. To know others well. To mend that which is broken. To reseed the barren desert."

The women lifted their eyes. Each serene face met the sunlight and felt its grace. The deep scars under their left eyes no longer burned.

The stillness spoke up and made itself heard.

Vaguely, the play *Beat Down* was trying again to resonate in the minds of those who had seen it and they struggled to connect the two.

"Yeah, I think it is like that play somehow. They pair-the same, the—uhh…"

A tireless woman in a bagger uni continued to press against the tensed belt of humanity gawking in closer for a better look. Her unexpected side trip had taken too long, the overthrow of the man with the shellacked shark on the wall had taken too long. He had put up quite a fight. She looked helplessly at the console live vidcasting in her hand. She was half a mile away from where they were. She stopped struggling. Tears welled to her eyes and she snatched them away. It was a hard moment. She knew she was going to be too late to help them and her heart was splitting in two. Wedged in the crowd, she could only watch in silent horror what was unfolding, like Cassandra before gates of Agamemnon's house. She pushed on, fighting anyway wild the charge she made.

There was a beat, a moment when the crowd, every single breath held, every eye transfixed, waited. Like a single heartbeat at the rim of the abyss.

The beat passed.

Soundlessly, the Dropcore discharged their weapons.

They were no marksmen, but each shot found its programmed target and with a deafening percussion through the heart and mind of each Spine and dropped them neatly to the ground. Not one agonized scream reached their lips. The cloaks fluttered in the gathering breeze. 330 women lay at the foot of the Lighthouse; their death was witnessed by hundreds of millions.

On the stage, Kitty Reed stood, mouth agape, and she would give an involuntary eulogy by speaking into the live mike, which also broadcast her dim, useless words.

"Oh my, we have a situation here at the lighthouse. I think that the Spine are dead. They were isolated by some sort of Footmen that I have never seen before." To wit, she added, "But Footmen don't shoot people so- I don't know-I'm Kitty Reed, here at the lighthouse, More later, in my newsports, sponsored by *Thin Banana, the thin banana for thin people and Coolwalk we walk with you, not against you.*"

The crowd looked at her hoping she'd continue. That didn't seem to fit what happened. They wanted something more, they felt a bit cheated, some would have used the word anger, since they did not yet know the word for rage. Someone threw a shoe at her. Someone else coughed and someone in the crowd began to moan. The uproar didn't come, but all were waiting for a spark to light their kindled spirits. Jernull pushed his way through the edge of the crowd, exhausted. He had been ahead of Hadorn, but it wasn't enough. He burst out from the crowd and fell forward. He regained himself and using a broadcast device in his hand, decommissioned all iso beams in the vicinity and the Dropcore themselves. The Dropcore sat down and began to beamcuff themselves as their instructions from Jernull's unit blared in their minds. He ran at and mounted the stage in a single jump. He jostled past the thunderstruck Kitty Reed and positioned himself before the vidcaster.

He tried to speak, and his voice cracked. He breathed in, set his jaw, and reminded himself that misinformation spreads quickly and early. He did not let his mind explore the possibility that one of the cloaks just beyond the stage belonged to Kenda. When he looked up to speak again, he spoke loudly and clearly and with all the nobility in him, "Something has happened here that will not go unanswered. Hundreds of women were just shot in plain view of millions of people. This act was done by the

Footmen at the command of my own paternal figure. He is currently in custody another offense, but he will also stand for this crime. This is not a time for anger. This is a time to act upon this outrage. But to act rightly, you need to know what happened. I vow as the new CEO of Bits and Bytes to tell you all that was behind what transpired here. You deserve to know. It will take some time to unravel these crucial seconds. I promise that it is owed to you and that it will be delivered. As my first official act as CEO, I am restructuring the newsporter protocol."

Users of the P_ear, saw a line splayed across their consciousness, *Corrupt Bits and Bytes Mogul Banburn Overthrown, Selected-progeny-heir steps in.* When the credits flashed to pay for the story, every hand keyed over the word *accept,* and they kept reading,

New format: Associated Wire Report by: Jernull Banburn...

"The Spine is not our enemy. They protected a very powerful Source. It is the human conversation through narrative; it is shared experience. The Spine was and still is in danger because my paternal figure had an interest in making us see them as villains. Interest makes people choose bad paths. In taking over the corporation, I promise that changes will be made to how newsporting is done. The new model being introduced today will put news consumption into the hands of the you-the reader. It will be built on a direct model. A direct model, previously thought untenable without advertisement sponsorships, was paid for by the end-user- all of you...this can work. It has worked before."

At the top of the Lighthouse Monument, removed, but not apart from the events below, Kenda felt her stomach heave. As she saw the women drop, a rictus of pain shot through her forcing her to her knees, she screamed inside her mind, and no sound came from her lips. This? This is the signal? Using the spyglass, she could see many of the older Spine violently ripped from their final circle. Tears jumped to her eyes and she felt the world swim.

She breathed in and out rapidly, "This can't be. Stun? That was Dropcore though. How did this happen? This was the sign they had planned all along? No! Calm down, I've got to calm down. What do I do? What do I do? The sign. I've got to do my duty."

Numbly, as if on automatic, she reached over and lifted the primary release lever, just as she'd promised she would upon seeing the sign below. She barely felt the newly oiled metal beneath her grinding the last stubborn gear into place. Eaves in the rooftop opened up to row after row of thin yellow sheets.

They were rectangular and in every size imaginable. They took wing as they were ushered off the metal panels in droves and they kept coming and coming, driven by the giant gears below.

They began blowing in a large fanning spiral and began a curling, shifting descent. This flock, this great sea of paypr, undulated in the morning breezes. Unleashed from the tower, they went down and then rose up again on the drafts of air from below. The endless mass churned off of the commemorative scaffolding where Kenda watched. Flying printed material soared, finally settling over the crowds below. Each stack flew, separating, turning and sailing on the breeze. They looked like wings waning and waxing in the yellow beams of the new found sunlight.

Packaged with the pages, data packets streamed code quick releases for every Emotional Transfer Grid, rendering them inactive immediately. Outstretched hands began to snag sheets from the millions descending. The disabling data packets were transmitted via every EEM and vidcast to receivers at home and in Drinkcoffee!! houses. Hearts and minds began working in tandem.

Thirsting eyes drank the printed words. They sought this with their own eyes, released from distortion of their mindscreens, with their own minds unburdened from ads, and with their hearts untouched by juiced emotion. Hearts and minds read together. Slowly, people began to collect in circles, like this was some great game, finding people who had pages like their pages, parts of stories from their stories.

Their world turned, more Funlights failed and the bright sky opened before them in tones of blue they had never seen. Birds flew up sat on the support beams of the overhead panels, nevermore lovely, raven black against the blue. Readers took in every word, living a hundred lifetimes from a thousand ages in a million worlds and...

...they gathered reasons why it was a sin to kill certain birds and why even birds in cages sing. They read the madness brought by birds sitting on chamber doors.

They peered in secret gardens, caught 22 reasons not to fight, and learned how to wear red letters and red badges.

They found no exits, declared independence, turned screws, lived in a cabin with an uncle, wore an iron mask, and won something called the West.

They contemplated a blade of grass and howled at injustice, even twice sought to right injustice from a jail cell. They pushed stones in futility and sought strangers in a plague. They experienced living like a bug and what it was like to be a bat. They became invisible and sought sanctuary. They ate dreams in the middle of the summer nights and tamed unruly Kates. They cradled cats, touched the souls of their feet and knew the word compassion.

They held all the world's a stage and sung songs of distant earth. They found a woman who waited 20 years for a man beset against the entire ocean. And they knew the word faith and love. They heard a wild call and furious sound. They sat with death in a carriage and rode toward forever.

They had expectations of grandeur and were eaten alive by streets with no name and street cars that had one. They became boys lost and watched things and worlds fall apart. They watched yellow women in wallpaper fall to madness. They watched rabbits run into shining wires and generations fall into night. They watched bands continue to play. They dug holes where hearts would be buried. They watched plans come to ruin by silent ponds outside Salinas and in wretched wards where silent brooms kept watch.
They watched strange fruit wither in the sun as dreams were put aside. And they learned the word rage. And they knew the word outrage.

Such were the words that assailed their eyes, like rivers as thought. Free at long last, they spilled in every direction, the ocean of humanity's works flowing over desert dry plains washing into new channels craving low grounds, spilling into and carving new landscapes.

They learned the words for evil, anger and the difference between benign and malignant and insidious and found ways those words could not only be paired, but compared.

Walls within their organic binders shook, and their chains fell off. The timing was impeccable. From the words of the heart, came the past, in which the lens of the mind formed the future. Heart and mind paired, at last.

Kenda could feel the sun blaze forth, burning her face and arms. *The carrots will grow so much better*, she thought absently. She watched as the copies of the organic payprs shot out above her in a graceful arc and then they flowed down to even more waiting minds.

From the railing, Kenda stared down at her beloved Spine on the ground. People began respectfully covering the bodies.

She wiped stinging tears from her eyes and let the lever creak back into its cradle. She slumped over, her heart heavy and her mind pounding, each beat sounding in the emptiness. So many of the Spine-gone. Isolated. It was then that she noticed among the rusted levers and bolts, a shining metal plaque that some Spine member had screwed into the flaking rusted side of the lighthouse; it was so bright against the flagging veneer:

For all who failed to understand its light.

Kenda choked, "All things flow from Source. But you didn't need to pay like this." She felt her heart begin to beat again, slowly, audibly, but there was something else beating there. It was faint-the sound of wings on the wind rising up from a wide, pulsing sea, under a full and constant sun.

❧The Net

Free special bulletin for citizen subscribers EEMed directly to end users from MerroWire Broadcasting, formerly Bits and Bytes-

"The widest net humanity ever designed covered us so completely that its dis-entangling and removal did not solve how it had inscribed itself on our hearts and twisted itself round our minds. That particular removal required a revolution. Revolution cannot be forced upon a populace. There must be something in trade. Even as our net was removed, we moved not, still feeling the ropes, even as they fell from our backs. This evil, which came to us in comfort, robbed us of our origins and our future, giving us a single, infinite moment of the present. A life cannot be held in suspension, it should not be lived in suspension. Comfort does not command the allegiance of humankind. It produces nothing. And so the Spine add to their own metaphor-no longer merely Spine, but the edge of something great, a handheld wonder, that which holds together the pages of the human conversation."

🐦 Epilogue

Kenda went out to visit the museum site often. Sometimes with Jernull, sometimes alone. Even Dayzee came sometimes with Hadorn at her side. Hadorn had become the most voracious contributor to The MerroWire. She had also been helping Dayzee write a broadcast meant to help others about her recovery from the Push.

In the days after the Lighthouse, Kenda mostly came to the museum blast site seeking solace in her mourning.

As she walked in the ash piles, she felt her grief slide over her like a shawl. The explosion that happened here was set off by the Consourcium. They believed that they had to protect the books, so they blew apart an empty museum. Before they blew it up, they had taken all the books into hiding.

Their belief in the importance of Source materials-was a belief she shared. She understood their desire to keep Source safe and whole. They could not abide losing centuries of the human conversation to an algorithm. However, it was this act that almost doomed Source to extinction.

As she gazed upon the wide greyblack expanse, she saw it for what it was- a sacrifice. The Spine had paid dearly to absolve this sin. Maybe that was warranted. In her grief, though, she couldn't bring herself to believe this. The only thing she knew for certain was that she needed to keep this area alive somehow. *This memory seeds other things. It must be preserved. It should be a place to remember. Without memory, we are sterile. We are seedless. We exist in death.*

She had wanted to memorialize their sacrifice, and she had finally thought of a way to do that. She had written a tribute to the Spine who had inspired her.

She walked to the edge of the blast radius and she found the gold shard. She polished a small area on it, and she took out a torch that allowed her to etch words into it. When she had finished, she stood back to read the words in its glinting surface.

The fallen-
We exist at the edge of their end.
They risked, they paid,
they saved-
stories of
unyielding blades,
scourges, schemes,
the world's compass,
the dread night,
and grindstone dreams.

"Whatever you do, don't let them take your books."

-Spine Manual